SANDITON

JANE AUSTEN was born in 1775 in the village of Steventon, Hampshire, the daughter of an Anglican clergyman. The Austens were cultured but not at all rich, though one of Austen's brothers was adopted by a wealthy relative. Other brothers followed professional careers in the church, the Navy, and banking. With the exception of two brief periods away at school, Austen and her elder sister Cassandra, her closest friend and confidante, were educated at home. Austen's earliest surviving work, written at Steventon while still in her teens, is dedicated to her family and close female friends. Between 1801 and 1809 Austen lived in Bath, where her father died in 1805, and in Southampton. In 1809, she moved with her mother, Cassandra, and their great friend Martha Lloyd to Chawton, Hampshire, her home until her death at Winchester in 1817. During this time, Austen published four of her major novels: *Sense and Sensibility* (1811), *Pride and Prejudice* (1813), *Mansfield Park* (1814), and *Emma* (1816), visiting London regularly to oversee their publication. Her two final novels, *Persuasion* and *Northanger Abbey*, were published posthumously in 1818. *Sanditon*, a new novel, was left unfinished at the time of her death.

KATHRYN SUTHERLAND is Professor of English Literature and Senior Research Fellow, St Anne's College, Oxford. Her recent publications include *Jane Austen's Textual Lives: From Aeschylus to Bollywood* (2005) and, with Marilyn Deegan, *Transferred Illusions: Digital Technology and the Forms of Print* (2009). She is the editor of *Jane Austen's Fiction Manuscripts: A Digital Edition* (2010) and the expanded print edition, 5 vols (2018). In the Oxford World's Classics series she has also published editions of Walter Scott's *Redgauntlet* and *Waverley*, of Adam Smith's *An Inquiry into the Nature and Causes of the Wealth of Nations*, of James Edward Austen-Leigh's *A Memoir of Jane Austen and Other Family Recollections*, and of Jane Austen's *Teenage Writings*.

OXFORD WORLD'S CLASSICS

*For over 100 years Oxford World's Classics have brought
readers closer to the world's great literature. Now with over
700 titles—from the 4,000-year-old myths of Mesopotamia to the
twentieth century's greatest novels—the series makes available
lesser-known as well as celebrated writing.*

*The pocket-sized hardbacks of the early years contained
introductions by Virginia Woolf, T. S. Eliot, Graham Greene,
and other literary figures which enriched the experience of reading.
Today the series is recognized for its fine scholarship and
reliability in texts that span world literature, drama and poetry,
religion, philosophy and politics. Each edition includes perceptive
commentary and essential background information to meet the
changing needs of readers.*

OXFORD WORLD'S CLASSICS

JANE AUSTEN

Sanditon

Edited with an Introduction and Notes by
KATHRYN SUTHERLAND

OXFORD
UNIVERSITY PRESS

OXFORD
UNIVERSITY PRESS

Great Clarendon Street, Oxford, OX2 6DP,
United Kingdom

Oxford University Press is a department of the University of Oxford.
It furthers the University's objective of excellence in research, scholarship,
and education by publishing worldwide. Oxford is a registered trade mark of
Oxford University Press in the UK and in certain other countries

© Editorial material Kathryn Sutherland 2019

The moral rights of the author have been asserted

First published as an Oxford World's Classics paperback 2019

Impression: 1

Published in the United States of America by Oxford University Press
198 Madison Avenue, New York, NY 10016, United States of America

British Library Cataloguing in Publication Data

Data available

Library of Congress Control Number: 2019939271

ISBN 978-0-19-884083-1

Printed and bound in Great Britain by
Clays Ltd, Elcograf S.p.A.

CONTENTS

INTRODUCTION

THE scene is set. A gentleman and lady (as yet unnamed) are travelling home from London to the south coast. They leave the main road to follow a rough, unmade track. Their carriage overturns. The gentleman scrambles out, helping his companion to safety. He finds he has sprained his ankle. The reason for their diversion: he is looking for a doctor. But the track leads nowhere. There is no road; there is no doctor—dead end on two counts. As beginnings go, this is not encouraging. As the beginning of a novel by Jane Austen, it upsets all our expectations, much like that overturned carriage. We know how her novels open, and it is not like this. Austen's openings are remarkably similar: biographical, descriptive, and static—a snapshot or tableau introducing a named family or family member, captured at a particular moment in their history before the action starts. Not only does this new novel open with movement, that movement is hazardous and observed with forensic detachment. Warm biographical detail is noticeably withheld. In its place, the reader is offered a police incident report: 'A Gentleman and Lady travelling from Tunbridge', 'The accident happened', 'their Driver', 'the said House', 'the said Proprietor' (pp. 3–4). Only one paragraph in, we know that *Sanditon* will be unlike any other novel Austen wrote.

Another gentleman, Mr Heywood, a farmer, witnesses the incident and comes to the assistance of the travellers. They spend the next fortnight, while the ankle heals, among the numerous Heywood family before continuing their journey, taking with them for an extended visit Miss Charlotte Heywood, 'a very pleasing young woman of two and twenty' (p. 14). By now we are into Chapter 2, the gentleman has become Mr Parker and the lady his wife, Mrs Parker, and his character, so enigmatically introduced, has been pretty much decided: he is 'an Enthusiast' (p. 11). Mr Parker's enthusiasm (a word with a keener edge then than now) borders upon delusion and is certainly obsessive in nature. His every waking moment, all his energy, and his fortune are dedicated to Sanditon, his home and the fishing village he means to transform into a fashionable health resort. Sanditon is to Mr Parker 'a second wife and four Children . . . hardly less Dear—and certainly more engrossing' (p. 12).

The seaside holiday was invented in the eighteenth century, with resorts springing up along England's extensive coastline, from Blackpool and Scarborough in the north to Brighton and Lyme Regis in the south, to take advantage of the fashion for salt-water bathing. Their attractions were boosted by influential treatises like Dr Richard Russell's *Dissertation Concerning the Use of Sea Water*, published in Latin in 1750 and quickly issued in English. Demand for his treatments (he recommended drinking as well as bathing in sea water for a range of glandular ailments) encouraged Russell to build in Brighton in the mid-1750s a substantial residence for the reception of patients.[1] By the early 1800s, medical and pseudo-medical books and pamphlets advised sea air and bathing for a surprising variety of diseases—Mr Parker's faith in their being 'nearly infallible . . . for every Disorder, of the Stomach, the Lungs or the Blood' (p. 13) scarcely exaggerates—and every tourist guidebook had its promotional paragraphs in praise of the unique health benefits of one particular resort or another. John Anderson, Physician to and Director of the General Sea-Bathing Infirmary at Margate, assured his readers, after extensive research among local guides, of bathing being considered 'a certain specific' 'for the bite of a mad dog and other rabid animals', warning that the patient might bark 'much like a dog' when first dipped into the sea.[2] As William Cowper, Austen's favourite poet, put it in 1782: 'all impatient of dry land, agree | With one consent to rush into the sea'.[3] By 1800 seaside holidays were here to stay.

Sanditon is a fictitious location on the Sussex coast, a rival in Mr Parker's besotted view to the longer-established neighbouring

[1] For more on Richard Russell (1689–1759), see the entry by John H. Farrant in the *Oxford Dictionary of National Biography* <http://www.oxforddnb.com/view/10.1093/ref:odnb/9780198614128.001.0001/odnb-9780198614128-e-56302> retrieved 12 Oct. 2018.

[2] John Anderson, *A Practical Essay on the Good and Bad Effects of Sea-Water and Sea-Bathing* (London, 1795), 38.

[3] William Cowper, 'Retirement', lines 523–4, in *Poems* (London, 1782), 284.

resorts of Brighton, Eastbourne, and Worthing. By the late eighteenth century, arguments for the superiority of the Sussex coast—its shelter from northerly winds, the luminosity of its air, and its sunny aspect—were well rehearsed. This is not the first time Austen has imagined her characters by the sea. In her fourth novel, *Emma* (1816), fearful, complaining Mr Woodhouse disputes with his elder daughter Isabella the pros and cons of two resorts—South End (on the Thames Estuary in Essex) and Cromer (in north-east Norfolk)—for health and sea bathing, their conversation only serving to make Emma, who has never seen the sea, 'envious and miserable' (ch. 12). We learn here, too, that it was at Weymouth, a south-coast resort, fashionable since George III patronized it in 1789, that Jane Fairfax first made the acquaintance of Frank Churchill. In Weymouth, Jane narrowly escaped drowning (ch. 19). In *Persuasion*, finished only months before *Sanditon*, and published posthumously in 1818, the seaside again proves dangerous when Louisa Musgrove's foolish leap from the stone breakwater or Cobb at Lyme Regis in Dorset leaves her concussed (ch. 12). Perilous, but exhilarating, too, the seaside elicits rare moments of sensuous delight in a writer who does not easily set aside her guard; like the eulogy to Lyme and its neighbour Charmouth, with

its sweet retired bay, backed by dark cliffs, where fragments of low rock among the sands make it the happiest spot for watching the flow of the tide, for sitting in unwearied contemplation;—the woody varieties of the cheerful village of Up Lyme, and, above all, Pinny, with its green chasms between romantic rocks . . . these places must be visited, and visited again. (*Persuasion*, ch. 11)

And they were visited again and again: at Lyme, Austen, a keen bather, declared the 'Bathing . . . so delightful . . . I believe I staid in rather too long'; and at nearby Dawlish and Sidmouth she enjoyed family holidays in the opening years of the new century.[4]

Lady bathers, like Austen, would use bathing machines, huts on wheels. Inside, they stripped off their clothes and the machine was

---

[4] *Jane Austen's Letters*, ed. Deirdre Le Faye, 4th edn (Oxford: Oxford University Press, 2011), 99 (to Cassandra Austen, 14 September 1804).

rolled down to the water, the bather entering the sea with the assistance of a local woman or 'dipper'. Tobias Smollett gives the best literary account of a bathing machine in *Humphry Clinker* (1771), a novel-in-letters describing a tour through Britain. He writes here of the bather as 'he', but in fact machines were designed primarily for the use of female bathers:

Imagine to yourself a small, snug, wooden chamber, fixed upon a wheel-carriage, having a door at each end, and on each side a little window above, a bench below—The bather, ascending into this apartment by wooden steps, shuts himself in, and begins to undress, while the attendant yokes a horse to the end next the sea, and draws the carriage forwards, till the surface of the water is on a level with the floor of the dressing-room, then he moves and fixes the horse to the other end—The person within being stripped, opens the door to the seaward, where he finds the guide ready, and plunges headlong into the water.[5]

If the seaside already represented for Austen a place of adventure, somewhere the female body might enjoy unusual permitted freedom and the imagination take flight, *Sanditon* is her only truly seaside novel; her only novel to absorb into its structure something of what the seaside has come to mean in later modern fiction—in works like Kate Chopin's *The Awakening* (1899), Penelope Fitzgerald's *The Bookshop* (1978), John Banville's *The Sea* (2005), Ian McEwan's *On Chesil Beach* (2007), and Sarah Perry's *The Essex Serpent* (2017). Seaside novels are not a single type. What they share is an understanding of the sea and shore as a place of longing and change, where we might find or lose ourselves. The place where land dissolves into sea, where, as Austen suggests, romantic scenery is the consequence of landslips and cataclysm, the seaside is a threshold or space between, a place of transformation and transcendence—especially of human reality in the face of nature's great unaccountability. The sensitive mind responds to limitless views of sea and sky, intimating new beginnings or something darker—dissolution and death. Either way, as

---

[5] Tobias Smollett, *The Expedition of Humphry Clinker*, 3 vols, 2nd edn (London, 1771), ii. 134–5.

the term 'sea change' suggests, the effect upon the self is powerful and mysterious; we are not the same after a visit to the seaside.

Nor is the world of *Sanditon* the same as it appeared in Austen's earlier novels. Austen is a writer whose perspective on society is acute and precisely contemporary, shaped by Britain's war with Revolutionary and Napoleonic France, a war that spanned almost the whole of her adult life (from its outbreak in 1793 to Waterloo in 1815). Wartime explains the defensiveness of her closely woven and tightly patrolled (even claustrophobic) village communities, and the sceptical eye turned upon landed gentry, like Sir Thomas Bertram in *Mansfield Park* (1814) and Sir Walter Elliot in *Persuasion*, whose action or inaction threatens the stability of the estate (for 'estate' read 'nation'). In *Persuasion*, and through the quiet characterization of its suffering heroine, Anne Elliot, Austen offered her most subtle study of war's domestic attrition; the price paid by those who wait at home. Now in *Sanditon*, begun eighteen months after Napoleon's final defeat at Waterloo, she describes a world opening up to change.

With their wide prospects across the Channel, England's south-coast resorts remained fashionable despite the long years of con-flict. In fact, their attractions (and dangers) for giddy teenagers like Lydia Bennet, who follows the militia to Brighton in Austen's second novel *Pride and Prejudice* (1813), were only enhanced by the presence of army garrisons and scarlet-coated officers. Lydia's soldier-fixation, a recognized condition at the time, and known as 'scarlet fever', would not be cured by a trip to the seaside. In Admiral Croft and Captain Frederick Wentworth, men whose advancement has been by virtue of merit and risk, not inherited land, *Persuasion* celebrated the Navy, the force in which the nation placed its trust for much of the war, and described in the novel's closing words as 'that profession which is, if possible, more distin-guished in its domestic virtues than in its national importance'. But with the end of war, Austen now intimates, a new kind of risk has emerged: in a volatile post-war climate of boom and bust the sailor's meritorious risk has been replaced by the sheer recklessness of landed men, like Mr Parker of Sanditon. Mr Parker is gambling a comfortable property 'which two or three

Generations had been holding and accumulating before him'
(pp. 11–12) by investing in leisure.

Mr Parker is a type of modern man, dislocated by years of war
and wishing to make the world anew. The reader is soon enlight-
ened as to the pertinence of the novel's opening paragraph: the
overturned carriage and Mr Parker's accident are the consequences
of ridiculous misjudgement. The topography of Sanditon, described
in what is for Austen unusual detail as Charlotte and the Parkers
approach it from inland, is equally informative. In a sheltered dip,
two miles from the sea, the little party passes the Parkers' old house
with its well-stocked garden and orchard, then comes the church
and the 'real village of Sanditon', scarcely more than a collection
of cottages and a few modest shops—a baker's and a shoemaker's
are mentioned. Ahead, a fork in the road descends in one direction
to a cluster of fishermen's houses and, in the other, it ascends a hill
that terminates in 'a steep, but not very lofty Cliff'. It is here on
the hilltop looking out to sea that, in the narrator's words, 'the
Modern began' (p. 24). The modern, the vision shared by Mr Parker
and his fellow speculators, so far includes the desirable amenities
of hotel, library, billiard room, milliner's shop, an esplanade
(Austen's intended meaning for the word 'Mall'), equipped with
two green benches, where the fashionable come to parade and be
seen, and a row of smart houses. In this her final work, Austen, as
decisively as Mr Parker, sets the country village behind her to face
the new-built development marching close to the cliff edge.

Austen's country village implied something permanent and
known,[6] its carefully culled families with their usual routines thrown
into excitement or confusion by the appearance of a stranger
or two: the cynical urbanite Crawfords in *Mansfield Park*; the
metrosexual Frank Churchill in *Emma*. In contrast, the transient
inhabitants of Sanditon are as changeful as its shoreline. The social
scene is widening; visitors, rapidly sketched in, who have drifted for
one reason or another to the fledgling resort, outnumber residents.

---

[6] In two letters Austen described the country village as her ideal fictional terrain. See
Letters, 287 (to Anna Austen, 9 September 1814)—'3 or 4 Families in a Country Village
is the very thing to work on'; and p. 326 (to James Stanier Clarke, 1 April 1816)—'such
pictures of domestic Life in Country Villages as I deal in'.

Among them are several more Parkers. While his sisters self-medicate for imaginary illnesses, fat-boy Arthur Parker slyly stuffs his face and coddles himself by the fire. Only the chance to ogle the two Beaufort girls tempts him to brave the July breezes muffled inside an overcoat, while they, equipped with the essential holiday accessories of harp and drawing pad, make the best of it at Sanditon because their means do not stretch to the more fashionable resorts of Worthing or Eastbourne. Clara Brereton, companion to Lady Denham, Sanditon's 'Great Lady', is relatively settled after a six-month stay. Beautiful and wretchedly poor, Clara is Charlotte's 'idea of a complete Heroine' (p. 33). But will she find a rival as love interest in the resort's latest arrival, the mixed-race heiress and hothouse flower Miss Lambe? Then there is Charlotte Heywood herself, the original and oddly styled 'visiting young Lady' (p. 15).

Equally new is the attention paid to a whole class of workaday characters, essential to the smooth running of gentry society but invisible in earlier novels: we hear of old Stringer and son, market gardeners, Jebb the milliner, William Heeley shoemaker, and old Sam who uncords the trunks at the hotel; at the library we see Miss Whitby 'with all her glossy Curls'. The names in the library subscription book (Dr and Mrs Brown, Lieutenant Smith R.N., Miss Scroggs) and those busy promoting Sanditon's success at a distance (Fanny Noyce, Miss Capper, Mrs Charles Dupuis) dissolve into an unusually thronged background. Everywhere there is variety, bustle, and life; and more of that life is lived out of doors, in the open air. With its dedication to pleasure and its spirit of optimism, Sanditon seems a place designed to upset expectations.

Lady Denham, Mr Parker's co-investor, is a new kind of authority figure for Austen: made powerful by money and strategic marriages rather than breeding. A ruthless property developer, without Mr Parker's anxiety to promote the prosperity of the whole community, her eye is for the main chance. Seventy, and in robust health, she means to exploit the illness, real and imaginary, that brings others to the sea. Sir Edward Denham, her second husband's penniless heir, and God's gift (so he thinks) to women, is a fortune hunter intent on seducing her young companion, Clara, who just might have the key to Lady Denham's fortune and stony heart. When she is not prescribing alarming remedies for herself and others, Miss Diana Parker is a meddlesome do-gooder pursuing charitable projects that call for insane levels of interference and energy. The Parker sisters, with their 'Zeal for being useful' (p. 55), are repeatedly described by their kind-hearted brother as 'excellent Women', the phrase surely borrowed by Barbara Pym for the title of her 1952 comedy of manners, *Excellent Women*, about the lives of equally busy post-war spinsters built around church jumble sales and good works. In manuscript, Austen revised her initial description of the Parker sisters' 'disease of activity' to the gentler phrasing of 'spirit of restless activity'. The Parkers, Charlotte Heywood concludes, 'were no doubt a family of Imagination' (p. 55). The diagnosis applies equally to Lady Denham and Sir Edward with their get-rich-quick schemes. These are not idlers by the seaside, indulging in holiday dreams of health, wealth, and romance, but seasoned fantasists. In one way or another, they are all speculators. Are they also dangerous?

Speculation of several kinds is set to be a major concern of the novel. Charlotte Heywood, for much of the narrative the reader's eyes and ears on events, is given to speculation as she processes the sights and sounds of a world she witnesses but never really enters. The effect is disorientating; she is repeatedly assailed by the new and the unexpected. In this resort filled with eccentrics, she must regularly reassess: did she really see/hear that? what can she/he mean by it? is this a kind or a cruel/an intelligent or a stupid person? A resort, like a cruise ship or a train, is a device beloved of detective fiction writers for bringing together an assortment of loosely or seemingly unconnected characters and setting them to act one with another—to reveal themselves. By presenting Charlotte as a problem solver, the novel's air of mystery is deepened.

But speculation takes a further precise form. As described by the economist Adam Smith, 'Sudden fortunes, indeed, are sometimes made . . . by what is called the trade of speculation'.[7] In this

---

[7] Adam Smith, *An Inquiry into the Nature and Causes of the Wealth of Nations*, 2 vols (London, 1776), i. 140 (Book 1, ch. 10). See, too, 'speculation', *OED*, sense 8a.

sense, speculation is the buying and selling of goods or land in order to profit by a rise or fall in the market rather than with the purpose of regular investment. It is taking a gamble in the hope of quick returns and without concern for the long-term effects on community or environment of what might simply be profiteering. In only twelve chapters, 'speculation' used in this sense appears six times and 'speculating' once. The 'two Post chaises', seen by Mr and Mrs Parker and Charlotte crossing the down to the hotel, and described as not only 'a joyful sight' but 'full of speculation' (p. 57), nicely conflates the imaginative and economic guesswork that occupies their several thoughts.

Readers are unlikely to associate Austen with the classical economic theory of her day, but a conversation between Mr Parker and Lady Denham, his 'Colleague in speculation' (p. 15), revises that assumption. They debate the effect of demand on supply and the consequences that a more general diffusion of wealth might bring for their local community. While he welcomes the prospect of free-spending visitors and the higher prices and increased production they might stimulate, she is jealous to protect her interests against servants wanting higher wages. Not only does this speak in timely fashion to the state of the national economy, in the grip of post-war depression, it sounds much like Jane Marcet's *Conversations on Political Economy* (1816), a work that successfully explained Smith's doctrines for a popular audience. Like Marcet, Austen here recognizes the significance of economic discourse, replacing an older argument based on mutual obligation, to the description of modern society; like Marcet, too, she brings political economy down to the domestic level and 'the price of our necessaries of Life' (p. 34).

Austen's novels have won appreciation for their naturalism—for the way she restricts the development and resolution of her romantic plots to something like the probable range of human behaviour. But there was always the whiff of sensationalism in her realist project, a flirtation with the wilder imagination and extravagant devices of pulp fiction—the stock-in-trade of the circulating library whose titles Catherine Morland devours in *Northanger Abbey* (1818) and that Sir Edward Denham here turns to for lifestyle advice. Debauchery, adultery, and other dark crimes lurk in the shadows of all Austen's plausible tales: not one but two ruined and abandoned Elizas in her first novel *Sense and Sensibility* (1811); Wickham's planned seduction of Georgiana Darcy at Ramsgate in *Pride and Prejudice*; Henry Crawford's callous destruction of married Maria Rushworth's reputation in *Mansfield Park*; the heartless behaviour of Mr William Elliot towards Mrs Smith, widow of the man he ruined, in *Persuasion*. The exaggeration and melodrama for which her contemporary William Wordsworth condemned the 'frantic' modern novel,[8] and which Austen indulges sparingly in the margins of her adult fiction, takes centre-stage in *Sanditon*. Among the consequences are a new freedom, openness, and energy. There is freedom in the absurd posturing of Sir Edward, whose passion for Walter Scott's verses brings the enigmatic declaration, 'That Man who can read them unmoved must have the nerves of an Assassin!—Heaven defend me from meeting such a Man un-armed' (p. 39). There is frustrated sexual energy in Miss Diana Parker's persistent rubbing, 'six Hours without Intermission', of Mrs Sheldon's coachman's ankle (p. 28). With *Sanditon* Austen is taking social realism into strange waters.

Most obviously strange is the novel's language. Communication breaks down under assault from the various projectors and imaginists,[9] each trapped inside their bizarre thought bubbles and unique speech habits. Mr Parker's impassioned niche marketing lends his enthusiastic riffs the puffed up style of a guidebook. Here he is extolling the therapeutic effects of the seaside:

The Sea Air and Sea Bathing together were nearly infallible, One or the other of them being a match for every Disorder, of the Stomach, the Lungs or the Blood; They were anti-spasmodic, anti-pulmonary, anti-sceptic, anti-bilious and anti-rheumatic. Nobody could catch cold by the Sea, Nobody wanted appetite by the Sea, Nobody wanted Spirits. Nobody wanted Strength.—They were healing, softing,

---

[8] 'Preface' (1800) to *Lyrical Ballads*, in *The Prose Works of William Wordsworth*, ed. W. J. B. Owen and Jane Worthington Smyser, 3 vols (Oxford: Clarendon Press, 1974), i. 128.

[9] 'A person who imagines something.' *Emma*, ch. 39: 'How much more must an imaginist, like herself, be on fire with speculation and foresight!' The *OED* credits Austen with one of the earliest uses of the term.

relaxing—fortifying and bracing—seemingly just as was wanted—some-
times one, sometimes the other.—If the Sea breeze failed, the Sea-
Bath was the certain corrective;—and where Bathing disagreed, the
Sea Breeze alone was evidently designed by Nature for the cure. (p. 13)

Here is a popular guidebook of the time, promoting sea air and
bathing at Brighton:

Those who use the cold or warm sea-bath, very soon become sensible
how much *the air of the coast* contributes to general health; indeed, in
almost every instance, its good effects are far more considerable than is
generally supposed. To the young, and those debilitated by years, its
influence is often surprising . . . to those in the vigour of life, the
stimulus deriveable from wine, or fermented liquors, is amply supplied
by the revivifying effects of sea air alone; so much so indeed, as to render their use, in most cases, quite unnecessary. To these general facts
may be added, the evidence arising from the health and vigour of the
resident inhabitants of the sea-shore, who are strangers to the melancholy catalogue of diseases which annually prevail in inland situations,
and who present numerous examples of unusual and vigorous old age.[10]

Sir Edward Denham has amassed a complete lexicon of hard,
shiny, new words which he lobs into the conversation to the considerable confusion of Charlotte Heywood and the reader. His
hyperbolic ravings on the anti-hero, his favourite character in the
contemporary novel—'T'were Pseudo-Philosophy to assert that
we do not feel more enwraped by the brilliancy of his Career, than
by the tranquil and morbid Virtues of any opposing Character'—
reduce Charlotte to the Alice-like observation: 'If I understand
you aright'—said Charlotte—'our taste in Novels is not at all the
same' (p. 46). Verbal idiosyncrasy signals a community that has
lost its connective glue—society falling apart. Sanditon is, after
all, the town built upon sand.

Linguistic and stylistic oddity is not confined to the novel's
eccentrics. Diana Parker's officious acts of charity inspire sympa-
thetic notes of insurgency in a narrator who, striving to keep pace
with her, describes her meddling in paramilitary terms: 'she was

---

[10] [John Feltham,] *A Guide to all the Watering and Sea-Bathing Places*, new and
improved edn (London, 1815), 130.

now regaling in the delight of opening the first Trenches of an acquaintance with such a powerful discharge of unexpected Obligation' (p. 57). Syllepsis or zeugma, whereby one verb governs two different, incongruous objects, a device Austen relished as a teenage writer, is again in evidence: 'Apply any Verses you like to it—But I want to see something applied to your Leg' (p. 8), says Mr Heywood, whom modest means oblige 'to be stationary and healthy' (p. 14).[11] The quirky angle of vision that persists through the novel is announced in its opening paragraph, where the travellers remain faceless while the road is given 'a most intelligent portentous countenance' (p. 3). Mystery is heightened by compressed or elliptical phrases: the description of Clara Brereton as 'a dependant on Poverty' (p. 18); of Miss Lambe as 'half-mulatto, chilly and tender' (p. 64); and of Charlotte's glimpse over the paling fence of 'something White and Womanish' (p. 70).

One of the oddest features of *Sanditon* is its unusual air of detachment. The distance between Charlotte Heywood and the seaside world she encounters and attempts to analyse is rarely bridged. And those who assume that Charlotte is the usual Austen heroine, aligned more closely than any other character with the narrator's perspective, should consider how little Austen relies in this her last novel on the kind of double voicing or intimacy with her heroine that colours *Emma* and *Persuasion*, and the almost equal interplay of the narrator's voice with that of Mr Parker, a leading eccentric. *Sanditon* reads like an experiment in testing the social basis of perception. How do we know who and what to trust? How will it all turn out?

We do not know. *Sanditon* was left unfinished; in some ways, it is barely begun. By her own dating of the first page, Austen started the new novel on 27 January 1817, setting it aside after twelve chapters, on 18 March 1817. Five days later she wrote to her niece Fanny Knight:

[11] In the short tale 'Jack & Alice' in the teenage writings 'cruel' Charles Adams has steel traps placed in the grounds of his estate, 'to wound the hearts & legs of all the fair' (Jane Austen, *Teenage Writings*, ed. Kathryn Sutherland and Freya Johnston (Oxford: Oxford University Press, 2017), 18).

I certainly have not been well for many weeks, & about a week ago I was very poorly . . . I must not depend upon being ever very blooming again. Sickness is a dangerous Indulgence at my time of Life.[12]

She died four months later on 18 July, aged forty-one, possibly from Addison's disease (at the time, undiagnosed and not in fact described before the mid-nineteenth century). In all, she wrote about 24,000 words of the new work, around one-fifth the length of her usual completed novels.

Unfinished works are not easily detached from their point of origin; author biography plays a special part in how we make sense of them. *Sanditon*, Austen's last novel, is a satire about the contemporary craze for seaside holidays; it is also a study of people who imagine they are ill, written by a woman we know was dying. To us she appears to be shadow boxing and laughing at death. Diana Parker, deluded hypochondriac and martyr to the same condition, 'spasmodic bile', as her author in her final months, reads like a mad alter ego. But did Austen know she was dying when she began to write? The novel is written in a radically new, impressionistic style. Was this deliberate or a distortion caused by illness? Is Austen striking out in a new direction or failing to establish overall control of a work which, had she been stronger, would have proceeded on more familiar lines? Unavoidable and unanswerable questions; every reader will ask them. As light and funny as it is, this fragment is Austen's most poignant work. More than anything else, it confirms the rightness of what we know was her final choice of subject. If the ground beneath her characters' feet appears less secure than in her previous novels, her own vision is opening out. Austen too looks out to sea—to new horizons, to new beginnings, and perhaps to endings.

Continuing Sanditon

Criticism has regularly drawn attention to the fragment's enigmatic qualities. *Sanditon* quickly departs from the well-rehearsed Austen

---

[12] *Letters*, 350–1 (23 March 1817).

story of a marriageable young heroine singled out (here on a visit
to the seaside) so that we might observe her encounters with several eligible young men, from the charming but worthless to the
ultimately worthy, whom she will come to love. In its place, we find
a more immediate and troubling preoccupation with a range of
eccentrics. With the focus on their behaviour rather than the heroine's, local embellishment appears to take precedence over steady
plotting; again, a sense of disconnection, which may be either
a comment on the holiday spirit inspiring the resort's transient
population or a sign of *Sanditon*'s broken structure. The unfinished novel was not published until 1925. As an early critic noted,
though 'a bold venture in a new way of telling a story' and 'an
advance beyond its predecessors, none of them would, if broken
off short at the eleventh chapter, have left us in such uncertainty
as to the way in which it was going to develop'.[13] E. M. Forster's
verdict in a 1925 review was far harsher: *Sanditon*, he wrote, 'gives
the effect of weakness . . . and we realize with pain that we are listening to a slightly tiresome spinster, who has talked too much in
the past to be silent unaided'.[14] To Margaret Drabble, another
novelist, introducing the work to the general reader in 1974, the
'rather unsympathetic, hard, unsubtle nature of the satire' is
'surely best explained by its author's state of health. She has
returned to an almost eighteenth-century view of man as a being
dominated by a ruling passion.'[15] Recent commentators continue
to sense both disintegration and what Tony Tanner called 'a new
kind of phenomenological complexity' in its development, described
by Clara Tuite as '[t]he elusive "newness" . . . as well as the para-
doxical "buoyancy" of this death-bed text'.[16] The range of interpretation (itself a witness to the imaginative power of unfinished

[13] Mary Lascelles, *Jane Austen and Her Art* (London: Oxford University Press, 1939), 39.

[14] E. M. Forster, reviewing Chapman's transcription of *Sanditon* in the *Nation*, 21 (March 1925); reprinted in *Abinger Harvest* (1936; Harmondsworth: Penguin, 1967), 167 and 168.

[15] *Lady Susan, The Watsons, Sanditon*, ed. Margaret Drabble (Harmondsworth: Penguin, 1974), 31.

[16] Tony Tanner, *Jane Austen* (Basingstoke: Macmillan, 1986), 282; and see Clara Tuite, *Romantic Austen: Sexual Politics and the Literary Canon* (Cambridge: Cambridge University Press, 2002), 158.

works) is perhaps greater than for any of the six printed novels. In short, is it a work of illness or bold experiment (or both)?

Of all the vistas and wide prospects lending *Sanditon* its unusual air of transcendence the most open is that suggested by its story. Nothing is determined; everything is possible. Any number of new characters might yet appear. Sidney Parker, already set up to be the one sane member of the Parker family, is on the point of arriving along with 'a friend or two' (p. 69). Will Sidney be the hero to Charlotte Heywood's clear-sighted heroine? Will theirs be the happy ending? Or will the plot develop along less predictable lines? The contents of Mrs Whitby's circulating library have inflamed the imagination of Sir Edward Denham, but everyone to some extent inhabits a private fantasy—even Charlotte, who persists, despite her own self-caution, in reading Clara Brereton's character as that of a romantic heroine. Will Clara be abducted and worse by Sir Edward as was her almost namesake Clarissa Harlowe by Robert Lovelace, Sir Edward's model, in Richardson's novel *Clarissa*? Or, even more sensationally, will the West Indian heiress Miss Lambe oust her as his victim? What further obstacles might Lady Denham throw in the way of her hopeful heirs? Will the story perhaps return to the 'very inferior part of London', home of those 'politic and lucky Cousins, who seemed always to have a spy on her'? (p. 18) The briefest hint of a backstory as summarized by Mr Parker on first describing Lady Denham, this surely deserves further development: the seedier districts of London to be contrasted with the sea and sun of Sanditon? And what by way of adventures and romance might the holiday licence of Sanditon itself produce? As well as the usual Austen fare of balls, picnics, and dinner parties, there is the opportunity to indulge the delights of nude bathing. Austen, we should remember, was a Regency writer, not a prim Victorian.

One of several fragments left in manuscript at her death in July 1817, *Sanditon* became the property of Austen's elder sister Cassandra. Cassandra guarded her sister's manuscripts as fiercely as she protected her reputation. Precious relics, they were divided between remaining family members after Cassandra's death in 1845, when *Sanditon* was inherited by their niece Anna Lefroy.

Anna was just six weeks old when her name was first associated
with Austen's writings, as the unwitting dedicatee of two miniature
mock-moral stories in her aunt's teenage notebook *Volume the
First*. Austen was at the time seventeen years old. By the time Anna
herself was seventeen, she and Aunt Jane had collaborated on several comic tales and, under Austen's supportive instruction, Anna
had begun a novel of her own, with the tentative title 'Which is the
Heroine?'. She would later claim that *Sanditon* emerged in part
from discussions she had with her aunt: 'members of the Parker
family (except of course Sidney) were certainly suggested by conversations which passed between Aunt Jane & me during the time
that she was writing this story'.[17]

Continuations are also acts of criticism, informing and altering
how we understand the original. Some time after 1845, Anna
Lefroy took up *Sanditon* and attempted to finish it. What she
wrote shows considerable confidence in assuming the subject and
voice of the original. Like Austen, she deploys the full canvas of
sky and sea and open countryside. She enlarges the indigenous
local community at the fishing cove of old Sanditon, where the
addition of a public house, the Hollis Arms, precursor of the modern hotel on the fashionable higher ground, nicely anticipates the
tensions that might emerge between the different social groups
occupying old village and new town. The graft is barely detectable
by which Hollis land and Hollis money are made to provide the
means for conjuring the further new builds of Denham Place,
Denham Villas, and Denham Gardens, as outlined in Lefroy's
opening sentences; they flow effortlessly from the closing words of
Austen's fragment:

Poor Mr Hollis!—It was impossible not to feel him hardly used; to be
obliged to stand back in his own House and see the best place by the fire
constantly occupied by Sir Harry Denham. (p. 71)

---

[17] Anna Lefroy to James Edward Austen-Leigh, 8 August 1862, Hampshire Record
Office, MS 23M93/86/3c, item 118. For Jane Austen's collaborations with her niece
Anna Austen (later Lefroy), see Kathryn Sutherland, *Jane Austen's Textual Lives: From
Aeschylus to Bollywood* (Oxford: Oxford University Press, 2005), 246–57. Deirdre Le
Faye, '*Sanditon*: Jane Austen's Manuscript and her Niece's Continuation', *Review of
English Studies*, NS 38 (1987), 56–71, provides a transcript of Anna's comments.

The influence of later years displayed it self beyond the Walls of Sanditon House: & whilst the Denham Place, & Denham Villas of modern Sanditon (with the Denham Gardens, which formed part of the original plan, & still made a good figure in the prospectus) were all situated on land belonging to the Hollis estate, it was only the little old way-side Public House, at the foot of the hill, just where a by-road turned off to the fishing Hamlet, that retained the name, as it had once done the sign, of 'The Hollis Arms'.[18]

Lefroy appreciates the fine absurdities of Austen's comic technique. She catches the rhythms of an Austenian sentence; for example, in handling the mood and scene shift occasioned by a change in the weather:

Before the end of the week there came a melancholy change of weather, & two stormy days & nights of cold continuous rain. Such is always a trying season for the pleasure-seekers of a bathing place, whose first object, after securing their Lodgings is to be as little with inside them as possible.[19]

It is her departures from Austen's text, however, that afford the greatest instruction. In Lefroy's version, the apparently submissive (in fact, quietly sceptical) Mrs Parker finds a voice, and it is disappointingly commonplace and sensible; Charlotte Heywood is made more directly complicit with the narrator, and both she and Sidney Parker lose their subtle critical edge and risk becoming merely 'good' characters. The outsider roles Austen appeared to prepare for them are taken over instead by a newcomer—Mr Tracy. Mr Tracy is a mysterious figure, sinister, described as 'an acute & very useful political agent, the probable reason of his living so much abroad'.[20] Some years previously, he had been of service in rescuing Sir Edward from a fleecing during his European tour. Tracy is a foil to Sidney Parker and, as an observer, less well intentioned than Charlotte Heywood. Most surprising of all, Clara Brereton,

---

[18] *Jane Austen's Sanditon: A Continuation by Her Niece*, ed. Mary Gaither Marshall (Chicago: The Chiron Press, 1983), 1.

[19] *Sanditon: A Continuation*, 49–50. The phrase 'with inside' is used by Austen in *Emma* (ch. 10).

[20] *Sanditon: A Continuation*, 35.

made 'cold, calculating, & selfish' by poverty, is revealed as a scheming fortune hunter ('Thankful & trustworthy in the common affairs of every day life, but capable of systematic deception'),[21] with a plan to relieve Lady Denham of her money; in a reversal, Sir Edward is to become her victim and not she his. But with all this preparation in place (in particular, an elaborate backstory for Clara), Lefroy's nerve failed her and she abandoned the continuation after one hundred and thirteen pages.

Lefroy's aborted attempt darkens the novel's mood. Set aside and left in manuscript, a revised working draft like her aunt's original, it was only published in 1983. By then, there had been further continuations. Nevertheless, and by virtue of its author's peculiar intimacy with the circumstances of Austen's writing, Lefroy's version holds a special place in the crowded sub-genre of Austen continuations and sequels. Alice Cobbett's *Somehow Lengthened* (1932) (the title is a Byron quotation) engrosses details from Austen's fragment into its opening chapters before going its own sensational way. That way involved heightening the fragment's Regency-style naughtiness. Not only Sir Edward Denham, but the West Indian heiress, now named Miss Lorelia Lambe, is discovered to have 'a positive Byron mania': 'so romantic! So handsome! So delightfully wicked and remorseful and icy and glowing!' she enthuses.[22] Further romantic embellishments see Sir Edward's home, Denham Place, a rendezvous and storehouse for local smugglers, who assist in his abduction of Clara. The novel ends in a duel and a marriage. Cobbett relishes the fun of the original but her continuation is wearyingly verbose and indeed somewhat too lengthened.

In contrast, *Sanditon*, by Jane Austen and Another Lady (1975), binds the fragment to a novel that follows, too slavishly, the general pattern of Austen's earlier works. In a postscript styled 'An Apology from the Collaborator', the 'Lady/Collaborator', Marie Dobbs (aka Anne Telscombe), defends her anodyne choices: 'Ever

[21] *Sanditon: A Continuation*, 81.

[22] Alice Cobbett, *Somehow Lengthened: A Development of 'Sanditon'* (London: Ernest Benn Ltd, 1932), 65.

increasing numbers, seeking to escape the shoddy values and cheap garishness of our own age, are turning to the past to catch a glimpse of life in what appear to be far more leisured times.' She has no doubt that Charlotte Heywood 'was clearly intended as the heroine' and Sidney Parker 'marked out for the hero'.[23] Why abandon a formula that worked? she asks, seemingly oblivious to the fact that Austen herself had ditched it. In Donald Measham's self-published novel, *Jane Austen Out of the Blue* (2006), the fragment's completion hangs upon the metafictional conceit that the seaside resort of Sanditon might breathe new life and opportunity into an assortment of characters from Austen's earlier fictions: *Pride and Prejudice*'s Elizabeth Bennet (now Mrs Darcy) gives birth to her first child at Sanditon; *Emma*'s Mr Woodhouse dies there, his body partly pickled in brine for the journey back home to Highbury; and, unlikeliest of all, Charlotte Heywood marries the foppish Robert Ferrars (of *Sense and Sensibility*).

Riotously, and with great panache, Reginald Hill's *A Cure for All Diseases* (2008), dedicated 'To Janeites everywhere', exploits to full quirky effect the humour of Austen's original, excavating and burnishing those elements of mystery and even crime that the fragment's earliest readers (Anna Lefroy among them) detected beneath its surface. Hill's own brand of wit and whimsy and acute character observation segues perfectly into Austen's. His title, a quotation from Sir Thomas Browne's *Religio Medici* (1642)—'We all labour against our own cure for death is the cure of all diseases'—is wonderfully apt, too, reminiscent of the defiant energy that sparks from Austen's last pages. Hill's novel features his regular police duo Dalziel and Pascoe: Superintendent Andy Dalziel is recuperating in the old-fashioned Yorkshire resort of Sandytown, 'Home of the Healthy Holiday'. Charlotte Heywood is a psychologist with a sceptical and scientific research interest in alternative therapies. Much married Lady Daphne Denham, the principal landowner, has plans to refurbish both town and local Avalon Clinic. As Mr Parker, her business partner in the Sandytown Development Consortium, points out, alternative therapies are 'another great

[23] Jane Austen and Another Lady, *Sanditon* (London: Peter Davies, 1975), 326–8.

21st century growth area'.[24] Then there are Lady Denham's heirs
circling greedily and hopefully. Murder (to be precise, strangling
and roasting) is not far away. Continuing with the detective genre,
itself an inevitable outgrowth of Austen's village fictions, Carrie
Bebris's *The Suspicion at Sanditon (Or, the Disappearance of Lady
Denham)* (2015) offers the seventh and last in a series of well-
received Mr and Mrs Darcy Mysteries which began with *Pride
and Prescience* (2004).

Professionally published and self-published print and e-book
continuations of Austen's works are now in competition with web-
based adaptations, films, and more. The multiplatform web series
Welcome to Sanditon (2013), a Pemberley Digital production,
relocates the action from the English south coast to a California
beach town and replaces Charlotte Heywood with Gigi (Georgiana)
Darcy from *The Lizzie Bennet Diaries* (2012–13). Gigi is in California
to test Domino, a new video-conferencing application. Fans of
this interactive adaptation are invited to play at being residents
of Sanditon, creating their own characters, and uploading videos.
Jennifer Petkus's ingenious *Jane, Actually; Or Jane Austen's Book
Tour* (2013) is set in the present day but includes Austen as a character. Petkus, a creator of 'websites for the dead' (AfterNet technology) and a writer of Austen-themed mysteries, here permits
Austen to complete *Sanditon* and, by means of an avatar (an acting
student called Mary Crawford), to go on a book-signing tour.[25]

Film versions of *Sanditon* have been late on the scene. Chris
Brindle's two-part adaptation of 2014 takes the form of a filmed
play and a documentary: the play based equally on the unfinished
versions of Austen and her niece Anna Lefroy; the documentary
taking in the story of Lefroy's writing of her continuation. A film
derived from Marie Dobbs's 1975 completion is advertised as
in production with Fluidity Films, directed by Jim O'Hanlon

---

[24] Reginald Hill, *A Cure for All Diseases* (London: HarperCollins, 2008), 16. The novel
is titled *The Price of Butcher's Meat* in the USA and Canada.

[25] Mary Gaither Marshall, 'Jane Austen's *Sanditon*: Inspiring Continuations,
Adaptations, and Spin-Offs for 200 Years', *Persuasions Online*, 38 (1) (Winter 2017), offers
the most comprehensive listing of these later continuations (http://www.jasna.org/
persuasions/on-line/index.html). For titles, see 'Further Reading' in this edition.

(director of the 2009 BBC four-part adaptation of Austen's *Emma*, starring Romola Garai) and with a screenplay by Simon Reade, who adapted *Pride and Prejudice* for the stage. And latest of all, *Sanditon* is brought to the television screen by Andrew Davies, more than twenty years after his iconic BBC miniseries *Pride and Prejudice*. Commissioned for ITV, the fragment's twelve short chapters are stretched to make eight hour-long episodes. If in Davies's re-imagination whole scenes were added to Austen's finished novel, most memorably to enhance Mr Darcy's eroticism, what greater licence does *Sanditon* encourage and even require?

Indeed, the oddest of the many odd features of Austen's final fragment is its ready cinematic style—its atmospheric seascapes; its panoramas of the South Downs, criss-crossed by walkers and carriages moving between village, beach, and new town; its character close-ups, more easily interpreted by film-watcher than novel-reader; its use of fragmented vision and discontinuity; its teasing, flirtatious play of surfaces. The lingering gaze of the camera can luxuriate in the outdoor locations and render them more picturesque; it can exaggerate the eccentricities of the resort's inhabitants and enhance the novel's air of mystery. Film can intensify the visual paradoxes that assail Charlotte, the outsider; the camera can assume her perspective. There is room to diversify the scene: the dingier parts of London and even the lush landscapes of the West Indies would not be out of place. The cast Austen assembled offers ample scope to inject further energy, absurdity, and Regency rakishness into this joyous and unexpected seaside tale of opportunists and fantasists set on making the world anew.

NOTE ON THE TEXT

SANDITON was left in manuscript at Jane Austen's death in July 1817. She wrote her novel into three small homemade booklets, filling 120 pages in all with around 24,000 words. The manuscript ends abruptly part way through Chapter 12. It has no title. Jane Austen's nephew, James Edward Austen-Leigh, first brought the unfinished novel to public attention when he issued a highly selective summary, together with a few quotations, under the title 'The Last Work', in the second edition of his *Memoir of Jane Austen* (1871). In 1925, more than a hundred years after Austen set it aside, R. W. Chapman published the first complete transcription, calling it *Fragment of a Novel*. According to family tradition, Austen's working title for the novel was 'The Brothers', but 'Sanditon' seems to have been an unofficial title, in use at least from the mid-nineteenth century.[1] Austen's original manuscript is now held at King's College, Cambridge. Another copy, made by her sister Cassandra Austen, is in Jane Austen's House Museum, Chawton, Jane Austen's home from 1809 to 1817 and the place where *Sanditon* was written. This remained Cassandra's home until her death in 1845. For ease of reading, and to honour its important status as the very first adaptation or performance of Austen's text, Cassandra's copy has been used to establish this edition. For those wishing to consult Austen's original manuscript, full photographic images are available with a transcription at the open access site http://www.janeausten.ac.uk

In terms of modern conventions for preparing a manuscript for other eyes, Austen's original text seems far from finished. There are very few paragraph divisions and the pages are peppered with

---

[1] James Edward Austen-Leigh, *A Memoir of Jane Austen, to which is added Lady Susan and fragments of two other unfinished tales by Miss Austen*, 2nd edn (London: Richard Bentley, 1871), 181–94; *Fragment of A Novel written by Jane Austen January–March 1817* [ed. R. W. Chapman] (Oxford: Clarendon Press, 1925). Janet Sanders, 'Sanditon', *Times Literary Supplement*, 19 February 1925, p. 120; Anna Lefroy refers to the work as 'Sanditon' in family letters in 1862 and 1869 (see *A Memoir of Jane Austen*, ed. Kathryn Sutherland (Oxford: Oxford University Press, 2002), 184).

abbreviations ('B^r' for 'Brother', 'c^d' for 'could', 'S' for 'Sanditon', 'Miss D. P.' for 'Miss Diana Parker', and many more). Such contractions contribute to the impressionistic energy of the work, but they do not make for ease of reading. Cassandra made her copy after 1831 (the date of the watermark in its paper). Like the original, it is without a title. Unlike the original, it is a corrected fair copy. Deletions and the evidence of heavy revision in the original are not preserved. Contractions are, in most cases, expanded: characters' names are written out in full, as are numbers; '&' becomes 'and'; 'c^d' becomes 'could', and so on. Speeches are carefully apportioned and given speech marks. The work is paragraphed throughout. Many of Austen's characteristic long dashes are removed, especially those that, in Cassandra's opinion, appeared to suggest paragraph breaks. The text flows smoothly. The present edition derives from Austen's original manuscript but, for ease of reading, adopts Cassandra's formatting decisions.

Cassandra also corrected a few obvious slips and offered clear readings for some points of ambiguity in the original. For example, in her opening paragraph Austen wrote: 'especially as the Carriage was not the Gentleman's own' before striking out 'not' and adding above the line 'not his Master's'. Modern editors have been unsure how to interpret this alteration, but Cassandra offers the reading: 'especially as the Carriage was not his Master's but the Gentleman's own', and this is adopted here (p. 3). In Chapter 6, Lady Denham mentions a 'Chamber-House' but only one line later Austen appears to correct this to a 'Chamber-Horse' (a form of exercise machine). Cassandra transcribed both instances as 'Chamber-Horse', and this is the reading followed here (p. 35). In Chapter 11, the narrator uses the phrase 'rototary motion' to describe the fashionable aspirations of the Miss Beauforts, eager to move in the right circles. Cassandra corrects this to 'rotatory motion' (p. 65); this alteration is also adopted.

The present edition does not adopt Cassandra's 'improvements' to Austen's spellings. When Austen wrote, spelling, especially in manuscript, was not standardized; variation was allowable. Spellings such as 'travellor', 'ancle', 'cheif', 'neice', 'veiw', 'yeild', 'beleive', 'medecine', 'medecinal' not only carry the stamp of

Austen's personality as a writer, they were used by other writers of the time. They have been allowed to remain; so too her irregular capitalization of initial letters of common nouns occurring mid-sentence—a common practice in writing of the time and in many cases preserved by Cassandra. In other respects, barring the odd copying error, Cassandra's transcription is identical with her sister's manuscript. In imitation of Jane Austen, she signed its last page '*J. A.*' and below added: '*Begun on the 27ᵗʰ Jan'y* | *Ceased on the 18ᵗʰ March 1817*'.

FURTHER READING

Editions

Fragment of a Novel written by Jane Austen January–March 1817 [ed. R. W. Chapman] (Oxford: Clarendon Press, 1925).

Jane Austen's Fiction Manuscripts: A Digital Edition, ed. Kathryn Sutherland (2010) http://www.janeausten.ac.uk (an open access resource containing full photographic images with transcriptions, descriptions, and provenance details for all Austen's fiction manuscripts). Austen's handwritten manuscript of *Sanditon* can be read here.

Textual Studies

Southam, Brian, *Jane Austen's Literary Manuscripts: A Study of the Novelist's Development through the Surviving Papers* (1964); revised edn (London: Athlone Press, 2001).

Southam, Brian, *Jane Austen: A Students' Guide to the Later Manuscript Works* (London: Concord Books, 2007).

Biography

Jane Austen's Letters, ed. Deirdre Le Faye, 4th edn (Oxford: Oxford University Press, 2011).

Austen-Leigh, James Edward, *A Memoir of Jane Austen and Other Family Recollections*, ed. Kathryn Sutherland, Oxford World's Classics (Oxford: Oxford University Press, 2002).

Byrne, Paula, *The Real Jane Austen: A Life in Small Things* (London: HarperPress, 2013) (ch. 18, 'The Bathing Machine').

Clery, E. J., *Jane Austen, The Banker's Sister* (London: Biteback Publishing, 2017).

Le Faye, Deirdre, *Jane Austen: A Family Record*, 2nd edn (Cambridge: Cambridge University Press, 2004).

Nokes, David, *Jane Austen. A Life* (London: Fourth Estate, 1997).

Tomalin, Claire, *Jane Austen. A Life* (Harmondsworth: Viking, 1997).

Criticism

Persuasions Online, 38 (2) (Spring 2018), the whole issue is dedicated to essays containing the most recent research on and critical readings of *Sanditon*: http://www.jasna.org/persuasions/on-line/index.html

Darcy, Jane, 'Jane Austen's *Sanditon*, Doctors, and the Rise of Seabathing', *Persuasions Online*, 38 (2) (Spring 2018).

Harris, Jocelyn, *Satire, Celebrity, and Politics in Jane Austen* (Lewisburg, PA: Bucknell University Press, 2017).

Jordan, Elaine, 'Jane Austen Goes to the Seaside: *Sanditon*, English Identity, and the "West Indian" Schoolgirl', in *The Postcolonial Jane Austen*, ed. You-me Park and Rajeswari Sunder Rajan (London: Routledge, 2000), 29–55.

Miller, D. A., *Jane Austen, or The Secret of Style* (Princeton: Princeton University Press, 2003), 76–92.

Sutherland, Kathryn, *Jane Austen's Textual Lives: From Aeschylus to Bollywood* (Oxford: Oxford University Press, 2005), 168–97.

Tanner, Tony, *Jane Austen* (Basingstoke: Macmillan, 1986) (ch. 8 offers a close criticism of *Sanditon*).

Tuite, Clara, *Romantic Austen: Sexual Politics and the Literary Canon* (Cambridge: Cambridge University Press, 2002) (ch. 4 discusses '*Sanditon* and the sexual politics of land speculation').

Wiltshire, John, *Jane Austen and the Body* (Cambridge: Cambridge University Press, 1992) (ch. 5 discusses '*Sanditon*: the enjoyments of invalidism').

Continuations

Marshall, Mary Gaither, 'Jane Austen's *Sanditon*: Inspiring Continuations, Adaptations, and Spin-Offs for 200 Years', *Persuasions Online*, 38 (1) (Winter 2017) offers the most comprehensive listing: http://www.jasna.org/persuasions/on-line/index.html

Austen, Jane, and Another Lady, *Sanditon* (London: Peter Davies, 1975).

Bebris, Carrie, *The Suspicion at Sanditon (Or, the Disappearance of Lady Denham): A Mr and Mrs Darcy Mystery* (New York: Tor, 2015).

Brindle, Chris, *Jane Austen's 'Sanditon': The Film of the Play* (2014) and *Jane Austen's 'Sanditon': Documentary* (2014), available as a 2 DVD set through Amazon UK; see http://www.sanditon.info

Bushman, Jay, and Dunlap, Margaret, *Welcome to Sanditon*, an interactive multiplatform website (Pemberley Digital Production, 2013–). http://www.pemberleydigital.com/welcome-to-sanditon

Cobbett, Alice, *Somehow Lengthened* (London: Ernest Benn Ltd, 1932).

Hill, Reginald, *A Cure for All Diseases* (London: HarperCollins, 2008) (titled *The Price of Butcher's Meat* in the USA and Canada).

Lefroy, Anna, *Jane Austen's Sanditon: A Continuation by Her Niece*, ed. Mary Gaither Marshall (Chicago: The Chiron Press, 1983).

Measham, Donald, *Jane Austen Out of the Blue* (No place: Lulu, 2006).

Petkus, Jennifer, *Jane, Actually: Or Jane Austen's Book Tour* (Denver: Mallard Sci-Fi, 2013). Kindle edition.

A CHRONOLOGY OF JANE AUSTEN

Life	*Historical and Cultural Background*
1775 (16 Dec.) born in Steventon, Hampshire, seventh child of Revd George Austen (1731–1805), Rector of Steventon and Deane, and Cassandra Austen, née Leigh (1739–1827).	American War of Independence begins.
1776	American Declaration of Independence; James Cook's third Pacific voyage.
1778	France enters war on side of American revolutionaries. Frances Burney, *Evelina*
1779 Birth of youngest brother, Charles (1779–1852); eldest brother, James (1765–1819), goes to St John's College, Oxford; distant cousin Thomas Knight II and wife, Catherine, of Godmersham in Kent, visit Steventon and take close interest in brother Edward (1767–1852).	Britain at war with Spain; siege of Gibraltar (to 1783); Samuel Crompton's spinning mule revolutionizes textile production.
1781 Cousin Eliza Hancock (thought by some to be natural daughter of Warren Hastings) marries Jean-François Capot de Feuillide in France.	Warren Hastings deposes Raja of Benares and seizes treasure from Nabob of Oudh.
1782 Austens put on first amateur theatricals at Steventon.	Frances Burney, *Cecilia*; William Gilpin, *Observations on the River Wye*; William Cowper, *Poems*
1783 JA, sister Cassandra (1773–1845), and cousin Jane Cooper are tutored by Mrs Cawley in Oxford then Southampton until they fall ill with typhoid fever; death of aunt Jane Cooper from typhoid; brother Edward formally adopted by the Knights; JA's mentor, Anne Lefroy, moves into neighbourhood.	American independence conceded at Peace of Versailles; Pitt becomes Prime Minister.

Life	*Historical and Cultural Background*
Performance of Sheridan's *The Rivals* at Steventon.	India Act imposes some parliamentary control on East India Company; Prince Regent begins to build Brighton Pavilion; death of Samuel Johnson.
1785 Attends Abbey House School, Reading, with Cassandra.	William Cowper, *The Task*
1786 Brother Francis (1774–1865) enters Royal Naval Academy, Portsmouth; brother Edward on Grand Tour (to 1790); JA and Cassandra leave school for good.	William Gilpin, *Observations, Relative Chiefly to Picturesque Beauty . . . particularly the Mountains, and Lakes of Cumberland, and Westmoreland*
1787 Starts writing stories collected in three notebooks (to 1793); cousin Eliza de Feuillide visits Steventon; performance of Susannah Centlivre's *The Wonder* at Steventon.	American constitution signed.
1788 JA and Cassandra taken on a trip to Kent and London; *The Chances* and *Tom Thumb* performed at Steventon; brother Henry (1771–1850) goes to St John's College, Oxford; brother Francis sails to East Indies on HMS *Perseverance*; cousins Eliza de Feuillide and Philadelphia Walter attend Hastings's trial.	Warren Hastings impeached for corruption in India; George III's first spell of madness.
1789 James and Henry in Oxford produce periodical, *The Loiterer* (to Mar. 1790); JA begins lifelong friendship with Martha Lloyd and sister Mary when their mother rents Deane Parsonage.	Fall of the Bastille marks beginning of French Revolution.
1790 (June) completes 'Love and Friendship'.	Edmund Burke, *Reflections on the Revolution in France*; [Mary Wollstonecraft], *Vindication of the Rights of Men*
1791 Brother Charles enters Royal Naval Academy, Portsmouth; (Nov.) completes 'The History of England'; Edward marries Elizabeth Bridges and they live at Rowling, Kent.	Parliament rejects bill to abolish slave trade. James Boswell, *Life of Johnson*; Ann Radcliffe, *The Romance of the Forest*

	Life	*Historical and Cultural Background*
1792	Writes 'Lesley-Castle' and 'Evelyn', and begins 'Kitty, or the Bower'; Lloyds leave Deane to make way for James and first wife, Anne Mathew; cousin Jane Cooper marries Capt. Thomas Williams, RN; sister Cassandra engaged to Revd Tom Fowle.	France declared a republic; Warren Hastings acquitted. Mary Wollstonecraft, *Vindication of the Rights of Woman*; Clara Reeve, *Plans of Education*
1793	Birth of eldest nieces, Fanny and Anna, daughters of brothers Edward and James; writes last of entries in the teenage notebooks; brother Henry joins Oxford Militia.	Execution of Louis XVI of France and Marie Antoinette: revolutionary 'Terror' in Paris; Britain declares war on France.
1794	Probably working on *Lady Susan*; cousin Eliza de Feuillide's husband guillotined in Paris.	Suspension of Habeas Corpus; 'Treason Trials' of radicals abandoned by government when juries refuse to convict; failure of harvests keeps food prices high. Uvedale Price, *Essays on the Picturesque*; Ann Radcliffe, *The Mysteries of Udolpho*
1795	Writes 'Elinor and Marianne' (first draft of *Sense and Sensibility*); death of James's wife; JA flirts with Tom Lefroy, as recorded in first surviving letter.	George III's coach stoned; Pitt's 'Two Acts' enforce repression of radical dissent.
1796	Visits Edward at Rowling; (Oct.) begins 'First Impressions'; subscribes to Frances Burney's *Camilla*.	Frances Burney, *Camilla*; Regina Maria Roche, *Children of the Abbey*; Jane West, *A Gossip's Story*
1797	Marriage of James to Mary Lloyd; (Aug.) completes 'First Impressions'; Cassandra's fiancé dies of fever off Santo Domingo; begins revision of 'Elinor and Marianne' into *Sense and Sensibility*; George Austen offers 'First Impressions' to publisher Cadell without success; Catherine Knight gives Edward possession of Godmersham; marriage of Henry and Eliza de Feuillide.	Napoleon becomes commander of French army; failure of French attempt to invade by landing in Wales; mutinies in British Navy, leaders hanged. Ann Radcliffe, *The Italian*

Life	*Historical and Cultural Background*
1798	Starts to write 'Susan' (later *Northanger Abbey*); visits Godmersham; death in driving accident of cousin Lady Williams (Jane Cooper).	Irish Rebellion; defeat of French fleet at Battle of the Nile; French army lands in Ireland; further suspension of Habeas Corpus. Elizabeth Inchbald, *Lovers' Vows*, translation of play by Kotzebue.
1799	Visit to Bath; probably finishes 'Susan'; aunt, Mrs Leigh-Perrot, charged with theft and imprisoned in Ilchester Gaol.	Napoleon becomes consul in France. Hannah More, *Strictures on the Modern System of Female Education*; Jane West, *A Tale of the Times*
1800	Stays with Martha Lloyd at Ibthorpe; trial and acquittal of Mrs Leigh-Perrot.	French conquer Italy; British capture Malta; food riots; first iron-frame printing press; copyright law extended to Ireland. Elizabeth Hamilton, *Memoirs of Modern Philosophers*
1801	Austens move to Bath on George Austen's retirement; James and family move into Steventon Rectory; first of series of holidays in West Country (to 1804), during one of which thought to have had brief romantic involvement with a man who later died; Henry resigns from Oxford Militia and becomes banker and Army agent in London.	Slave rebellion in Santo Domingo led by Toussaint L'Ouverture; Nelson defeats Danes at Battle of Copenhagen; Act of Union joins Britain and Ireland. Maria Edgeworth, *Belinda*
1802	Visits Godmersham; accepts, then the following morning refuses, proposal of marriage from Harris Bigg-Wither; revises 'Susan'.	L'Ouverture's slave rebellion crushed by French; Peace of Amiens with France; founding of William Cobbett's *Political Register*.
1803	With brother Henry's help, 'Susan' sold to publishers Crosby & Co. for £10.	Resumption of war with France.
1804	Starts writing *The Watsons*; (Dec.) death of Anne Lefroy in riding accident.	
1805	(Jan.) death of George Austen; stops working on *The Watsons*.	Battle of Trafalgar. Walter Scott, *The Lay of the Last Minstrel*

Life	*Historical and Cultural Background*
1806	Austens leave Bath; visit relations at Adlestrop and Stoneleigh; Martha Lloyd becomes member of Austen household after death of her mother; brother Francis marries Mary Gibson; JA, Cassandra, and Mrs Austen take lodgings with them in Southampton.	French blockade of continental ports against British shipping; first steam-powered textile mill opens in Manchester. Lady Morgan, *The Wild Irish Girl*
1807	Brother Charles marries Fanny Palmer in Bermuda.	France invades Portugal; slave-trading by British ships outlawed. George Crabbe, *Poems*
1808	JA visits Godmersham; death of Edward's wife Elizabeth after giving birth to eleventh child.	France invades Spain; beginning of Peninsular War. Debrett, *Baronetage* (*Peerage* first published 1802). Hannah More, *Coelebs in Search of a Wife*; Walter Scott, *Marmion*
1809	(Apr.) attempts unsuccessfully to make Crosby publish 'Susan', writing under pseudonym 'Mrs Ashton Dennis' ('M.A.D.'); visits Godmersham; (July) moves, with Cassandra, Martha, and Mrs Austen, to house owned by Edward at Chawton, Hampshire.	British capture Martinique and Cayenne from France.
1810	Publisher Egerton accepts *Sense and Sensibility*.	British capture Guadeloupe, last French West Indian colony; riots in London in support of parliamentary reform. Walter Scott, *The Lady of the Lake*
1811	(Feb.) begins *Mansfield Park*; stays with Henry and Eliza in London to correct proofs of *Sense and Sensibility*; (Oct.) *Sense and Sensibility*, 'by a Lady', published on commission; revises 'First Impressions' into *Pride and Prejudice*.	Prince of Wales becomes Regent; Luddite anti-machine riots in North and Midlands. Mary Brunton, *Self-Control*
1812	Copyright of *Pride and Prejudice* sold to Egerton for £110; Edward's family take name of Knight at death of Catherine Knight.	United States declare war on Britain; French retreat from Moscow; Lord Liverpool becomes Prime Minister after assassination of Spencer Perceval.

Life	*Historical and Cultural Background*
1813	(Jan.) *Pride and Prejudice* published to great acclaim; JA stays in London to nurse Eliza; death of Eliza; in letter, expresses her hatred for Prince Regent; (June) finishes *Mansfield Park*; second editions of *Sense and Sensibility* and *Pride and Prejudice*.	British invasion of France after Wellington's success at Battle of Vittoria. Byron, *The Giaour, The Bride of Abydos*; Robert Southey, *Life of Nelson*
1814	(21 Jan.) begins *Emma*; (Mar. and Nov.) visits brother Henry in London, sees Kean play Shylock; (May) Egerton publishes *Mansfield Park* on commission, sold out in six months; death of Fanny Palmer Austen, brother Charles's wife, after childbirth; marriage of niece Anna Austen to Ben Lefroy.	Napoleon defeated and exiled to Elba; George Stevenson builds first steam locomotive; Edmund Kean's first appearance at Drury Lane. Mary Brunton, *Discipline*; Frances Burney, *The Wanderer*; Byron, *The Corsair*; Maria Edgeworth, *Patronage*; Walter Scott, *Waverley*
1815	(29 Mar.) completes *Emma*; (Aug.) begins *Persuasion*; invited to dedicate *Emma* to the Prince Regent; visits Henry in London; (Dec.) *Emma* published by Murray.	Napoleon escapes; finally defeated at Battle of Waterloo and exiled to St Helena; Humphry Davy invents miners' safety lamp.
1816	'Susan' bought back from Crosby and revised as 'Catherine'; failure of Henry's bank; second edition of *Mansfield Park*; (Aug.) JA completes *Persuasion*; health beginning to fail.	Post-war slump inaugurates years of popular agitation for political and social reform.
1817	(Jan.–Mar.) works on *Sanditon*; (Apr.) makes her Will; moves, with Cassandra, to Winchester, to be closer to skilled medical care; (15 July) composes last poem 'When Winchester Races'; (18 July, 4.30 a.m.) dies in Winchester; buried in Winchester Cathedral; (Dec.) publication (dated 1818) of *Northanger Abbey* and *Persuasion*, together with brother Henry's 'Biographical Notice'.	Attacks on Prince Regent at opening of Parliament; death of his only legitimate child, Princess Charlotte.

SANDITON

CHAPTER 1

A GENTLEMAN and Lady travelling from Tunbridge towards that part of the Sussex Coast which lies between Hastings and East-Bourne,* being induced by Business to quit the high road, and attempt a very rough Lane, were overturned in toiling up its long ascent half rock, half sand.—The accident happened just beyond the only Gentleman's House near the Lane—a House, which their Driver on being first required to take that direction, had conceived to be necessarily their object, and had with most unwilling Looks been constrained to pass by—. He had grumbled and shaken his shoulders so much indeed, and pitied and cut his Horses so sharply, that he might have been open to the suspicion of overturning them on purpose (especially as the Carriage was not his Master's but the Gentleman's own) if the road had not indisputably become considerably worse than before, as soon as the premises of the said House were left behind—expressing with a most intelligent portentous countenance that beyond it no wheels but cart wheels could safely proceed.

The severity of the fall was broken by their slow pace and the narrowness of the Lane, and the Gentleman having scrambled out and helped out his companion, they neither of them at first felt more than shaken and bruised. But the Gentleman had in the course of the extrication sprained his foot—and soon becoming sensible of it, was obliged in a few moments to cut short, both his remonstrance to the Driver and his congratulations to his wife and himself—and sit down on the bank, unable to stand.

'There is something wrong here,' said he—putting his hand to his ancle—'But never mind, my Dear—(looking up at her with a smile)—It could not have happened, you know, in a better place.—Good out of Evil—. The very thing perhaps to be wished for. We shall soon get releif.—*There*, I fancy lies my cure'—pointing to the neat-looking end of a Cottage, which was seen romantically situated among wood on a high Eminence at some little Distance—'Does not *that* promise to be the very place?'

His wife fervently hoped it was—but stood, terrified and anxious, neither able to do or suggest anything—and receiving her first real comfort from the sight of several persons now coming to their assistance. The accident had been discerned from a Hayfield adjoining the House they had passed—and the persons who approached, were a well-looking Hale, Gentlemanlike Man, of middle age, the Proprietor of the Place, who happened to be among his Haymakers at the time, and three or four of the ablest of them summoned to attend their Master—to say nothing of all the rest of the field, Men, Women and Children—not very far off.

Mr. Heywood, such was the name of the said Proprietor, advanced with a very civil salutation—much concern for the accident—some surprise at any body's attempting that road in a Carriage—and ready offers of assistance. His courtesies were received with Good-breeding and Gratitude and while one or two of the Men lent their help to the Driver in getting the Carriage upright again, the Travellor said—'You are extremely obliging Sir, and I take you at your word.—The injury to my Leg is I dare say very trifling, but it is always best in these cases to have a Surgeon's opinion without loss of time; and as the road does not seem at present in a favourable state for my getting up to his house myself, I will thank you to send off one of these good People for the Surgeon.'*

'The Surgeon Sir!'—replied Mr. Heywood—'I am afraid you will find no Surgeon at hand here, but I dare say we shall do very well without him.'

'Nay Sir, if *he* is not in the way, his Partner will do just as well—or rather better—. I would rather see his Partner indeed—I would prefer the attendance of his Partner.—One of these good people can be with him in three minutes I am sure. I need not ask whether I see the House; (looking towards the Cottage) for excepting your own, we have passed none in this place, which can be the Abode of a Gentleman.'

Mr. Heywood looked very much astonished—and replied—'What Sir! are you expecting to find a Surgeon in that Cottage?—We have neither Surgeon nor Partner in the Parish I assure you.'

'Excuse me Sir'—replied the other. 'I am sorry to have the appearance of contradicting you—but though from the extent of the Parish or some other cause you may not be aware of the fact;—Stay—Can I be mistaken in the place?—Am I not in Willingden?—Is not this Willingden?'

'Yes Sir, this is certainly Willingden.'

'Then Sir, I can bring proof of your having a Surgeon in the Parish—whether you may know it or not. Here Sir—(taking out his Pocket book—) if you will do me the favour of casting your eye over these advertisements, which I cut out myself from the Morning Post and the Kentish Gazette,* only yesterday morning in London—I think you will be convinced that I am not speaking at random. You will find it an advertisement Sir, of the dissolution of a Partnership in the Medical Line—in your own Parish—exten- sive Business—undeniable Character—respectable references— wishing to form a separate Establishment—you will find it at full length Sir'—offering him the two little oblong extracts.

'Sir'—said Mr. Heywood with a good humoured smile—'if you were to shew me all the Newspapers that are printed in one week throughout the Kingdom, you would not persuade me of there being a Surgeon in Willingden,—for having lived here ever since I was born, Man and Boy fifty-seven years, I think I must have *known* of such a person, at least I may venture to say that he has not *much Business*—To be sure, if Gentlemen were to be often attempting this Lane in Post-chaises,* it might not be a bad Speculation for a Surgeon to get a House at the top of the Hill.—But as to that Cottage, I can assure you Sir that it is in fact—(inspite of its spruce air at this distance—) as indifferent a double Tenement as any in the Parish, and that my Shepherd lives at one end, and three old women at the other.' He took the peices of paper as he spoke—and having looked them over, added—'I beleive I can explain it Sir.—Your mistake is in the place.—There are two Willingdens in this Country—and your advertisements refer to the other—which is Great Willingden, or Willingden Abbots, and lies seven miles off, on the other side of Battel—quite down in the Weald. And *we* Sir—' (speaking rather proudly) 'are not in the Weald.'

'Not *down* in the Weald I am sure Sir,' replied the Travellor, pleasantly. 'It took us half an hour to climb your Hill.—Well

Sir—I dare say it is as you say, and I have made an abominably stupid Blunder.—All done in a moment;—the advertisements did not catch my eye till the last half hour of our being in Town;—when everything was in the hurry and confusion which always attend a short stay there—One is never able to complete anything in the way of Business you know till the Carriage is at the door—and accordingly satisfying myself with a breif enquiry, and finding we were actually to pass within a mile or two of a *Willingden*, I sought no farther.—My Dear—' (to his wife) 'I am very sorry to have brought you into this Scrape. But do not be alarmed about my Leg. It gives me no pain while I am quiet,—and as soon as these good people have succeeded in setting the Carriage to rights and turning the Horses round, the best thing we can do will be to measure back our steps into the Turnpike road* and proceed to Hailsham, and so Home, without attempting anything farther.—Two hours take us home, from Hailsham—And when once at home, we have our remedy at hand you know.—A little of our own Bracing Sea Air will soon set me on my feet again.—Depend upon it my Dear, it is exactly a case for the Sea. Saline air and immersion* will be the very thing.—My Sensations tell me so already.'

In a most friendly manner Mr. Heywood here interposed, entreating them not to think of proceeding till the ancle had been examined, and some refreshment taken, and very cordially pressing them to make use of his House for both purposes.

'We are always well stocked,' said he, 'with all the common remedies for Sprains and Bruises—and I will answer for the pleasure it will give my wife and daughters to be of service to you and this Lady in every way in their power.'

A twinge or two, in trying to move his foot disposed the Travellor to think rather more as he had done at first of the benefit of immediate assistance—and consulting his wife in the few words of 'Well my Dear, I beleive it will be better for us.'—turned again to Mr. Heywood—and said—'Before we accept your Hospitality Sir,—and in order to do away with any unfavourable impression which the sort of wild goose-chase you find me in, may have given rise to—allow me to tell you who we are. My name is Parker.—Mr.

Parker of Sanditon; this Lady, my wife Mrs. Parker.—We are on our road home from London;—*My* name perhaps—tho' I am by no means the first of my Family, holding Landed Property in the Parish of Sanditon, may be unknown at this distance from the Coast—but Sanditon itself—everybody has heard of Sanditon,—the favourite—for a young and rising Bathing-place, certainly the favourite spot of all that are to be found along the Coast of Sussex;—the most favoured by Nature, and promising to be the most chosen by Man.'

'Yes—I have heard of Sanditon.' replied Mr. Heywood—'Every five years, one hears of some new place or other starting up by the Sea, and growing the fashion.—How they can half of them be filled, is the wonder! *Where* People can be found with Money or Time to go to them!—Bad things for a Country;—sure to raise the price of Provisions and make the Poor good for nothing—as I dare say you find, Sir.'

'Not at all Sir, not at all'—cried Mr. Parker eagerly. 'Quite the contrary I assure you.—A common idea—but a mistaken one. It may apply to your large, overgrown Places, like Brighton, or Worthing, or East Bourne—but *not* to a small Village like Sanditon, precluded by its size from experiencing any of the evils of Civilization, while the growth of the place, the Buildings, the Nursery Grounds,* the demand for every thing, and the sure resort of the very best Company, those regular, steady, private Families of thorough Gentility and Character, who are a blessing everywhere, excite the industry of the Poor and diffuse comfort and improvement among them of every sort.—No Sir, I assure you, Sanditon is not a place——'

'I do not mean to take exceptions to *any* place in particular Sir,' answered Mr. Heywood—'I only think our Coast is too full of them altogether—But had not we better try to get you'—

'Our Coast too full'—repeated Mr. Parker—'On that point perhaps we may not totally disagree;—at least there are *enough*. Our Coast is abundant enough; it demands no more.—Every body's Taste and every body's finances may be suited—And those good people who are trying to add to the number, are in my opinion excessively absurd, and must soon find themselves the Dupes of their own fallacious Calculations.—Such a place as Sanditon Sir, I may say was wanted, was called for.—Nature had marked it out—had spoken in most intelligible Characters—The finest, purest Sea Breeze on the Coast—acknowledged to be so—Excellent Bathing—fine hard Sand—Deep Water ten yards from the Shore—no Mud—no Weeds—no slimey rocks—Never was there a place more palpably designed by Nature for the resort of the Invalid—the very Spot which Thousands seemed in need of.— The most desirable distance from London! One complete, measured mile nearer than East Bourne. Only conceive Sir, the advantage of saving a whole Mile, in a long Journey. But Brinshore Sir, which I dare say you have in your eye—the attempts of two or three speculating People* about Brinshore, this last year, to raise that paltry Hamlet, lying, as it does between a stagnant marsh, a bleak Moor and the constant effluvia* of a ridge of putrifying sea weed, can end in nothing but their own Disappointment. What in the name of Common Sense is to *recommend* Brinshore?—A most insalubrious Air—Roads proverbially detestable—Water Brackish beyond example, impossible to get a good dish of Tea within three miles of the place—and as for the Soil—it is so cold and ungrateful that it can hardly be made to yeild a Cabbage.—Depend upon it Sir, that this is a faithful Description of Brinshore—not in the smallest degree exaggerated—and if you have heard it differently spoken of——'

'Sir I never heard it spoken of in my Life before,' said Mr. Heywood. 'I did not know there was such a place in the World.'

'You did not!—There my Dear'—(turning with exultation to his Wife)—'you see how it is. So much for the Celebrity of Brinshore!—This Gentleman did not know there was such a place in the World.—Why, in truth Sir, I fancy we may apply to Brinshore, that line of the Poet Cowper* in his description of the religious Cottager, as opposed to Voltaire—"*She*, never heard of half a mile from home."'

'With all my Heart Sir—Apply any Verses you like to it—But I want to see something applied to your Leg—and I am sure by your Lady's countenance that she is quite of my opinion and thinks it a pity to lose any more time—And here come my Girls to

speak for themselves and their Mother. (two or three genteel looking young women, followed by as many Maid servants, were now
seen issueing from the House)—I began to wonder the Bustle
should not have reached *them*.—A thing of this kind soon makes
a Stir in a lonely place like ours.—Now Sir, let us see how you can
be best conveyed into the House.'

The young Ladies approached and said every thing that was
proper to recommend their Father's offers; and in an unaffected
manner calculated to make the Strangers easy—And as Mrs.
Parker was exceedingly anxious for releif—and her Husband by
this time, not much less disposed for it—a very few Civil Scruples
were enough—especially as the Carriage being now set up, was
discovered to have received such Injury on the fallen side as to be
unfit for present use.—Mr. Parker was therefore carried into the
House, and his Carriage wheeled off to a vacant Barn.

CHAPTER 2

THE acquaintance, thus oddly begun, was neither short nor unimportant. For a whole fortnight the Travellors were fixed at Willingden; Mr. Parker's sprain proving too serious for him to move sooner.—He had fallen into very good hands. The Heywoods were a thoroughly respectable family, and every possible attention was paid in the kindest and most unpretending manner, to both Husband and wife. *He* was waited on and nursed, and *she* cheered and comforted with unremitting kindness—and as every office of Hospitality and friendliness was received as it ought—as there was not more good will on one side than Gratitude on the other—nor any deficiency of generally pleasant manners on either, they grew to like each other in the course of that fortnight, exceedingly well.

Mr. Parker's Character and History were soon unfolded. All that he understood of himself, he readily told, for he was very openhearted;—and where he might be himself in the dark, his conversation was still giving information, to such of the Heywoods as could observe.—By such he was perceived to be an Enthusiast;*—on the subject of Sanditon, a complete Enthusiast.—Sanditon,—the success of Sanditon as a small, fashionable Bathing Place was the object, for which he seemed to live. A very few years ago, and it had been a quiet Village of no pretensions; but some natural advantages in its position and some accidental circumstances having suggested to himself, and the other principal Land Holder, the probability of its becoming a profitable Speculation, they had engaged in it, and planned and built, and praised and puffed, and raised it to a Something of young Renown—and Mr. Parker could now think of very little besides.

The Facts, which in more direct communication, he laid before them were that he was about five and thirty—had been married,—very happily married seven years—and had four sweet Children at home;—that he was of a respectable Family, and easy though not large fortune;—no Profession—succeeding as eldest son to the Property which two or three Generations had been holding and accumulating before him;—that he had two Brothers and two Sisters—all single and all independant—the eldest of the two former indeed, by collateral Inheritance,* quite as well provided for as himself.—His object in quitting the high road, to hunt for an advertising Surgeon, was also plainly stated;—it had not proceeded from any intention of spraining his ancle or doing himself any other Injury for the good of such Surgeon—nor (as Mr. Heywood had been apt to suppose) from any design of entering into Partnership with him—; it was merely in consequence of a wish to establish some medical Man at Sanditon, which the nature of the Advertisement induced him to expect to accomplish in Willingden.—He was convinced that the advantage of a medical Man at hand would very materially promote the rise and prosperity of the Place—would in fact tend to bring a prodigious influx;—nothing else was wanting. He had *strong* reason to beleive that *one* family had been deterred last year from trying Sanditon on that account—and probably very many more—and his own Sisters who were sad Invalids, and whom he was very anxious to get to Sanditon this Summer, could hardly be expected to hazard themselves in a place where they could not have immediate medical advice.

Upon the whole, Mr. Parker was evidently an amiable, family-man, fond of Wife, Children, Brothers and Sisters—and generally kind-hearted;—Liberal, gentlemanlike, easy to please;—of a sanguine turn of mind, with more Imagination than Judgement. And Mrs. Parker was as evidently a gentle, amiable, sweet tempered Woman, the properest wife in the World for a Man of strong Understanding, but not of capacity to supply the cooler reflection which her own Husband sometimes needed, and so entirely waiting to be guided on every occasion, that whether he were risking his Fortune or spraining his Ancle, she remained equally useless.—Sanditon was a second wife and four Children to him—hardly less Dear—and certainly more engrossing.—He could talk of it for ever.—It had indeed the highest claims;—not only those of Birthplace, Property, and Home,—it was his Mine, his Lottery, his Speculation and his Hobby Horse;* his Occupation his Hope and his Futurity.—He was extremely desirous of drawing his good friends at Willingden thither; and his endeavours in the cause, were as grateful and disinterested, as they were warm.—He wanted to secure the promise of a visit—to get as many of the Family as his own house would contain, to follow him to Sanditon as soon as possible—and healthy as they all undeniably were—foresaw that every one of them would be benefited by the sea.—He held it indeed as certain, that no person could be really well, no person, (however upheld for the present by fortuitous aids of exercise and spirits in a semblance of Health) could be really in a state of secure and permanent Health without spending at least six weeks by the Sea every year.—The Sea Air and Sea Bathing together were nearly infallible, One or the other of them being a match for every Disorder, of the Stomach, the Lungs or the Blood; They were anti-spasmodic, anti-pulmonary, anti-sceptic, anti-bilious and anti-rheumatic.* Nobody could catch cold by the Sea, Nobody wanted appetite by the Sea, Nobody wanted Spirits. Nobody wanted Strength.—They were healing, softing, relaxing—fortifying and bracing—seemingly just as was wanted—sometimes one, sometimes the other.—If the Sea breeze failed, the Sea-Bath was the certain corrective;—and where Bathing disagreed, the Sea Breeze alone was evidently designed by Nature for the cure.

His eloquence however could not prevail. Mr. and Mrs. Heywood never left home. Marrying early and having a very numerous Family, their movements had been long limited to one small circle; and they were older in Habits than in Age.—Excepting two Journeys to London in the year, to receive his Dividends, Mr. Heywood went no farther than his feet or his well-tried old Horse could carry him, and Mrs. Heywood's Adventurings were only now and then to visit her Neighbours, in the old Coach which had been new when they married and fresh lined on their Eldest Son's coming of age ten years ago.

They had very pretty Property—enough, had their family been of reasonable Limits to have allowed them a very gentlemanlike share of Luxuries and Change—enough for them to have indulged in a new Carriage and better roads, an occasional month at Tunbridge Wells, and symptoms of the Gout and a Winter at Bath;—but the maintenance, Education and fitting out of fourteen Children

demanded a very quiet, settled, careful course of Life—and
obliged them to be stationary and healthy at Willingden. What
Prudence had at first enjoined, was now rendered pleasant by
Habit. They never left home, and they had a gratification in saying
so.—But very far from wishing their Children to do the same,
they were glad to promote *their* getting out into the World, as
much as possible. *They* staid at home, that their Children *might* get
out;—and while making that home extremely comfortable, wel-
comed every change from it which could give useful connections
or respectable acquaintance to Sons or Daughters. When Mr. and
Mrs. Parker therefore ceased from soliciting a family-visit, and
bounded their veiws to carrying back one Daughter with them, no
difficulties were started. It was general pleasure and consent.

Their invitation was to Miss Charlotte Heywood, a very pleasing young woman of two and twenty, the eldest of the Daughters
at home, and the one, who under her Mother's directions had been
particularly useful and obliging to them; who had attended them
most, and knew them best.—Charlotte was to go,—with excellent
health, to bathe and be better if she could—to receive every
possible pleasure which Sanditon could be made to supply by
the gratitude of those she went with—and to buy new Parasols,
new Gloves, and new Broches, for her Sisters and herself at the
Library,* which Mr. Parker was anxiously wishing to support.—All that Mr. Heywood himself could be persuaded to
promise was, that he would send everyone to Sanditon, who asked
his advice, and that nothing should ever induce him (as far as the
future could be answered for) to spend even five shillings* at
Brinshore.

CHAPTER 3

Every Neighbourhood should have a Great Lady.—The great Lady of Sanditon, was Lady Denham; and in their Journey from Willingden to the Coast, Mr. Parker gave Charlotte a more detailed account of her, than had been called for before.—She had been necessarily often mentioned at Willingden,—for being his Colleague in speculation, Sanditon itself could not be talked of long, without the introduction of Lady Denham and that she was a very rich old Lady, who had buried two Husbands, who knew the value of Money, was very much looked up to and had a poor Cousin living with her, were facts already well known, but some further particulars of her history and her Character served to lighten the tediousness of a long Hill, or a heavy bit of road, and to give the visiting young Lady a suitable knowledge of the Person with whom she might now expect to be daily associating.

Lady Denham had been a rich Miss Brereton, born to Wealth but not to Education. Her first Husband had been a Mr. Hollis, a man of considerable Property in the Country, of which a large share of the Parish of Sanditon, with Manor and Mansion House made a part. He had been an elderly Man when she married him;—her own age about thirty.—Her motives for such a Match could be little understood at the distance of forty years, but she had so well nursed and pleased Mr. Hollis, that at his death he left her everything—all his Estates, and all at her Disposal.

After a widowhood of some years, she had been induced to marry again. The late Sir Harry Denham, of Denham Park in the Neighbourhood of Sanditon had succeeded in removing her and her large Income to his own Domains, but he could not succeed in the veiws of permanently enriching his family, which were attributed to him. She had been too wary to put anything out of her own Power—and when on Sir Harry's Decease she returned again to her own House at Sanditon, she was said to have made this boast to a friend 'that though she had *got* nothing but her Title from the Family, still she had *given* nothing for it.'

For the Title, it was to be supposed that she had married—and Mr. Parker acknowledged there being just such a degree of value for it apparent now, as to give her conduct that natural explanation. 'There is at times,' said he—'a little self-importance—but it is not offensive;—and there are moments, there are points, when her Love of Money is carried greatly too far. But she is a goodnatured Woman, a very goodnatured Woman,—a very obliging, friendly Neighbour; a chearful, independant, valuable character.—and her faults may be entirely imputed to her want of Education. She has good natural Sense, but quite uncultivated.—She has a fine active mind, as well as a fine healthy frame for a Woman of seventy, and enters into the improvement of Sanditon with a spirit truly admirable—though now and then, a Littleness *will* appear. She cannot look forward quite as I would have her—and takes alarm at a trifling present expence, without considering what returns it *will* make her in a year or two. That is—we think *differently*, we now and then, see things *differently*, Miss Heywood—Those who tell their own Story you know must be listened to with Caution.—When you see us in contact, you will judge for yourself.'

Lady Denham was indeed a great Lady beyond the common wants of Society—for she had many Thousands a year to bequeath, and three distinct sets of People to be courted by; her own relations, who might very reasonably wish for her Original Thirty Thousand Pounds among them, the legal Heirs of Mr. Hollis, who must hope to be more endebted to *her* sense of Justice than he had allowed them to be to *his*, and those Members of the Denham Family, whom her second Husband had hoped to make a good Bargain for.—By all of these, or by Branches of them, she had no doubt been long, and still continued to be, well attacked;—and of these three divisions, Mr. Parker did not hesitate to say that Mr. Hollis' Kindred were the *least* in favour and Sir Harry Denham's the *most*.—The former he beleived, had done themselves irremediable harm by expressions of very unwise and unjustifiable resentment at the time of Mr. Hollis's death;—the Latter, to the advantage of being the remnant of a Connection which she certainly valued, joined those of having been known to her from their Childhood, and of being always at hand to preserve their interest by reasonable attention. Sir Edward, the present Baronet, nephew to Sir Harry, resided constantly at Denham Park; and Mr. Parker had little doubt, that he and his Sister Miss Denham who lived with him, would be principally remembered in her Will. He sincerely hoped it.—Miss Denham had a very small provision—and her Brother was a poor Man for his rank in Society.

'He is a warm friend to Sanditon'—said Mr. Parker—'and his hand would be as liberal as his heart, had he the Power.—He would be a noble Coadjutor!*—As it is, he does what he can—and is running up a tasteful little Cottage Ornée,* on a strip of Waste Ground Lady Denham has granted him, which I have no doubt we shall have many a Candidate for, before the end even of *this* Season.'

Till within the last twelvemonth, Mr. Parker had considered Sir Edward as standing without a rival, as having the fairest chance of succeeding to the greater part of all that she had to give—but there was now another person's claims to be taken into the account, those of the young female relation, whom Lady Denham had been induced to receive into her Family.

After having always protested against any such addition, and long and often enjoyed the repeated defeats she had given to every attempt of her relations to introduce this young Lady, or that young Lady as a Companion at Sanditon House, she had brought back with her from London last Michaelmas* a Miss Brereton, who bid fair by her Merits to vie in favour with Sir Edward, and to secure for herself and her family that share of the accumulated Property which they had certainly the best right to inherit.—Mr. Parker spoke warmly of Clara Brereton, and the interest of his Story increased very much with the introduction of such a Character. Charlotte listened with more than amusement now;—it was solicitude and Enjoyment, as she heard her described to be lovely, amiable, gentle, unassuming, conducting herself uniformly with great good Sense, and evidently gaining by her innate worth, on the affections of her Patroness.—Beauty, Sweetness, Poverty and Dependance, do not want the imagination of a Man to operate upon. With due exceptions—Woman feels for Woman very promptly and compassionately.

Mr Parker gave the particulars which had led to Clara's admission at Sanditon, as no bad exemplification of that mixture of Character, that union of Littleness with Kindness with Good Sense with even Liberality which he saw in Lady Denham—After having avoided London for many years, principally on account of these very Cousins, who were continually writing, inviting and tormenting her, and whom she was determined to keep at a distance, she had been obliged to go there last Michaelmas with the certainty of being detained at least a fortnight.—She had gone to an Hotel—living by her own account as prudently as possible, to defy the reputed expensiveness of such a home, and at the end of three Days calling for her Bill, that she might judge of her state.—Its amount was such as determined her on staying not another hour in the House, and she was preparing in all the anger and perturbation which a beleif of very gross imposition *there*, and an ignorance of where to go for better usage, to leave the Hotel at all hazards, when the Cousins, the politic and lucky Cousins, who seemed always to have a spy on her, introduced themselves at this important moment, and learning her situation, persuaded her to accept such a home for the rest of her Stay as their humbler house in a very inferior part of London, could offer.—She went; was delighted with her welcome and the hospitality and attention she received from every body—found her good Cousins the Breretons beyond her expectation worthy people—and finally was impelled by a personal knowledge of their narrow Income and pecuniary difficulties, to invite one of the girls of the family to pass the Winter with her. The invitation was to *one*, for six months—with the probability of another being then to take her place;—but in *selecting* the one, Lady Denham had shewn the good part of her Character—for passing by the actual *daughters* of the House, she had chosen Clara, a Neice—, more helpless and more pitiable of course than any— a dependant on Poverty—an additional Burthen on an encumbered Circle—and one, who had been so low in every worldly veiw, as with all her natural endowments and powers, to have been preparing for a situation little better than a Nursery Maid.

Clara had returned with her—and by her good sense and merit had now, to all appearance secured a very strong hold in Lady

Denham's regard. The six months had long been over—and not a syllable was breathed of any change, or exchange.—She was a general favourite;—the influence of her steady conduct and mild, gentle Temper was felt by everybody. The prejudices which had met her at first in some quarters, were all dissipated. She was felt to be worthy of Trust—to be the very companion who would guide and soften Lady Denham—who would enlarge her mind and open her hand.—She was as thoroughly amiable as she was lovely—and since having had the advantage of their Sanditon Breezes, that Loveliness was complete.

CHAPTER 4

'AND whose very snug-looking Place is this?'—said Charlotte, as in a sheltered Dip within two miles of the Sea, they passed close by a moderate-sized house, well fenced and planted, and rich in the Garden, Orchard and Meadows which are the best embellishments of such a Dwelling. 'It seems to have as many comforts about it as Willingden.'

'Ah'—said Mr. Parker—'This is my old House—the house of my Forefathers—the house where I and all my Brothers and Sisters were born and bred—and where my own three eldest Children were born—where Mrs. Parker and I lived till within the last two years—till our new House was finished.—I am glad you are pleased with it.—It is an honest old Place—and Hillier keeps it in very good order. I have given it up you know to the Man who occupies the cheif of my Land. *He* gets a better House by it—and I, a rather better situation!—one other Hill brings us to Sanditon—modern Sanditon—a beautiful Spot.—Our Ancestors, you know always built in a hole.—Here were we, pent down in this little contracted Nook, without Air or Veiw, only one mile and three quarters from the noblest expanse of Ocean between the South foreland and the Land's end, and without the smallest advantage from it. You will not think I have made a bad exchange, when we reach Trafalgar House—which by the bye, I almost wish I had not named Trafalgar—for Waterloo is more the thing now. However, Waterloo is in reserve—and if we have encouragement enough this year for a little Crescent to be ventured on—(as I trust we shall) then, we shall be able to call it Waterloo Crescent*—and the name joined to the form of the Building, which always takes, will give us the command of Lodgers—. In a good Season we should have more applications than we could attend to.'

'It was always a very comfortable House'—said Mrs. Parker—looking at it through the back window with something like the fondness of regret.—'And such a nice Garden—such an excellent Garden.'

'Yes, my Love, but *that* we may be said to carry with us.—*It* supplies us, as before, with all the fruit and vegetables we want; and we have in fact all the comfort of an excellent Kitchen Garden, without the constant Eyesore of its formalities; or the yearly nuisance of its decaying vegetation.—Who can endure a Cabbage Bed in October?'

'Oh! dear—yes—We are quite as well off for Gardenstuff as ever we were—for if it is forgot to be brought at any time, we can always buy what we want at Sanditon-House.—The Gardiner there, is glad enough to supply us—. But it was a nice place for the Children to run about in. So Shady in Summer!'

'My dear, we shall have shade enough on the Hill and more than enough in the course of a very few years;—The Growth of my Plantations is a general astonishment. In the mean while we have the Canvas Awning, which gives us the most complete comfort within doors—and you can get a Parasol at Whitby's for little Mary at any time, or a large Bonnet at Jebb's—and as for the Boys, I must say I would rather *them* run about in the Sunshine than not. I am sure we agree my dear, in wishing our Boys to be as hardy as possible.'

'Yes indeed, I am sure we do—and I will get Mary a little Parasol, which will make her as proud as can be. How Grave she will walk about with it, and fancy herself quite a little Woman.—Oh! I have not the smallest doubt of our being a great deal better off where we are now. If we any of us want to bathe, we have not a quarter of a mile to go.—But you know, (still looking back) one loves to look at an old friend, at a place where one has been happy.—The Hilliers did not seem to feel the Storms last Winter at all.—I remember seeing Mrs. Hillier after one of those dreadful Nights, when *we* had been literally rocked in our bed, and she did not seem at all aware of the Wind being anything more than common.'

'Yes, yes—that's likely enough. *We* have all the Grandeur of the Storm, with less real danger, because the Wind meeting with nothing to oppose or confine it around our House, simply rages and passes on—while down in this Gutter—nothing is known of the state of the Air, below the Tops of the Trees—and the Inhabitants may be taken totally unawares, by one of those dreadful Currents which do more mischeif in a Valley, when they *do* arise than an open Country ever experiences in the heaviest Gale.—But my dear Love—as to Gardenstuff;—you were saying that any accidental omission is supplied in a moment by Lady Denham's Gardiner—but it occurs to me that we ought to go elsewhere upon such occasions—and that old Stringer and his son have a higher claim. I encouraged him to set up—and am afraid he does not do very well—that is, there has not been time enough yet.—He *will* do very well beyond a doubt—but at first it is Uphill work; and therefore we must give him what Help we can—and when any Vegetables or fruit happen to be wanted—and it will not be amiss to have them often wanted, to have something or other forgotten most days;—Just to have a nominal supply you know, that poor old Andrew may not lose his daily Job—but in fact to buy the cheif of our consumption of the Stringers.—'

'Very well my Love, that can be easily done—and Cook will be satisfied—which will be a great comfort, for she is always complaining of old Andrew now, and says he never brings her what she wants.—There—now the old House is quite left behind.—What is it, your Brother Sidney says about it's being a Hospital?'

'Oh! my dear Mary, merely a Joke of his. He pretends to advise me to make a Hospital of it. He pretends to laugh at my Improvements. Sidney says any thing you know. He has always said what he chose of and to us, all. Most Families have such a member among them I beleive Miss Heywood.—There is a someone in most families privileged by superior abilities or spirits to say anything.—In ours, it is Sidney; who is a very clever young Man,—and with great powers of pleasing.—He lives too much in the World to be settled; that is his only fault.—He is here and there and every where. I wish we may get him to Sanditon. I should like to have you acquainted with him.—And it would be a fine thing for the Place!—Such a young Man as Sidney, with his neat equipage* and fashionable air,—You and I Mary, know what effect it might have: Many a respectable Family, many a careful Mother, many a pretty Daughter, might it secure us, to the prejudice of East Bourne and Hastings.'

They were now approaching the Church and real village of Sanditon, which stood at the foot of the Hill they were afterwards to ascend—a Hill, whose side was covered with the Woods and enclosures of Sanditon House and whose Height ended in an open Down where the new Buildings might soon be looked for. A branch only, of the Valley, winding more obliquely towards the Sea, gave a passage to an inconsiderable Stream, and formed at its mouth, a third Habitable Division, in a small cluster of Fisherman's Houses.

The Village contained little more than Cottages, but the Spirit of the day had been caught, as Mr. Parker observed with delight to Charlotte, and two or three of the best of them were smartened up with a white Curtain and 'Lodgings to let'—, and farther on, in the little Green Court of an old Farm House, two Females in elegant white were actually to be seen with their books and camp stools—and in turning the corner of the Baker's shop, the sound of a Harp might be heard through the upper Casement.—Such sights and sounds were highly Blissful to Mr. Parker—Not that he had any personal concern in the success of the Village itself; for considering it as too remote from the Beach, he had done nothing there—but it was a most valuable proof of the increasing fashion of the place altogether. If the *Village* could attract, the Hill might be nearly full.—He anticipated an amazing Season.—At the same time last year, (late in July) there had not been a single Lodger in the Village!—nor did he remember any during the whole Summer, excepting one family of children who came from London for sea air after the hooping Cough, and whose Mother would not let them be nearer the shore for fear of their tumbling in.

'Civilization, Civilization indeed!'—cried Mr. Parker, delighted—. 'Look my dear Mary—Look at William Heeley's windows.—Blue Shoes, and nankin Boots!*—Who would have expected such a sight at a Shoemaker's in old Sanditon!—This is new within the month. There was no blue Shoe when we passed this way a month ago.—Glorious indeed!—Well, I think I *have* done something in my Day.—Now, for our Hill, our health-breathing Hill.—'

In ascending, they passed the Lodge-Gates of Sanditon House, and saw the top of the House itself among its Groves. It was the last Building of former Days in that line of the Parish. A little higher up, the Modern began; and in crossing the Down,

a Prospect House, a Bellevue Cottage, and a Denham Place were
to be looked at by Charlotte with the calmness of amused Curiosity,
and by Mr. Parker with the eager eye which hoped to see scarcely
any empty houses.—More Bills at the Window than he had calculated on;—and a smaller shew of company on the Hill—Fewer
Carriages, fewer Walkers. He had fancied it just the time of day for
them to be all returning from their Airings to dinner—But the
Sands and the Terrace always attracted some—. and the Tide
must be flowing—about half-Tide now.—He longed to be on the
Sands, the Cliffs, at his own House, and everywhere out of his
House at once. His Spirits rose with the very sight of the Sea and
he could almost feel his Ancle getting stronger already.

Trafalgar House, on the most elevated spot on the Down was
a light elegant Building, standing in a small Lawn with a very
young plantation round it, about an hundred yards from the brow
of a steep, but not very lofty Cliff—and the nearest to it, of every
Building, excepting one short row of smart-looking Houses, called
the Terrace, with a broad walk in front, aspiring to be the Mall
of the Place. In this row were the best Milliner's shop and the
Library—a little detached from it, the Hotel and Billiard
Room—Here began the Descent to the Beach, and to the Bathing
Machines*—and this was therefore the favourite spot for Beauty
and Fashion.—At Trafalgar House, rising at a little distance
behind the Terrace, the Travellors were safely set down, and all
was happiness and Joy between Papa and Mama and their Children;
while Charlotte having received possession of her apartment,
found amusement enough in standing at her ample, venetian window,* and looking over the miscellaneous foreground of unfinished Buildings, waving Linen, and tops of Houses, to the Sea,
dancing and sparkling in sunshine and Freshness.

CHAPTER 5

WHEN they met before dinner, Mr. Parker was looking over Letters.—'Not a Line from Sidney!'—said he.—'He is an idle fellow.—I sent him an account of my accident from Willingden, and thought he would have vouchsafed me an Answer.—But perhaps it implies that he is coming himself.—I trust it may.—But here is a Letter from one of my Sisters. *They* never fail me.— Women are the only Correspondents to be depended on.—Now Mary, (smiling at his Wife)—before I open it, what shall we guess as to the state of health of those it comes from—or rather what would Sidney say if he were here?—Sidney is a saucy fellow, Miss Heywood—And you must know, he will have it there is a good deal of Imagination in my two Sisters' complaints—but it really is not so—or very little—They have wretched health, as you have heard us frequently say, and are subject to a variety of very serious Disorders.—Indeed, I do not beleive they know what a day's health is;—and at the same time, they are such excellent useful Women and have so much energy of character that, where any Good is to be done, they force themselves on exertions which to those who do not thoroughly know them, have an extraordinary appearance.—But there is really no affectation about them. They have only weaker constitutions and stronger minds than are often met with, either separate or together.—And our youngest Brother—who lives with them, and who is not much above twenty, I am sorry to say, is almost as great an Invalid as themselves.—He is so delicate that he can engage in no Profession.—Sidney laughs at him—but it really is no Joke—though Sidney often makes me laugh at them all inspite of myself.—Now, if he were here, I know he would be offering odds, that either Susan, Diana or Arthur would appear by this Letter to have been at the point of death within the last month.'

Having run his eye over the Letter, he shook his head and began 'No chance of seeing them at Sanditon I am sorry to say.—A very indifferent account of them indeed. Seriously, a *very* indifferent account.—Mary, you will be quite sorry to hear how ill they have been and are.—Miss Heywood, if you will give me leave, I will read Diana's Letter aloud.—I like to have my friends acquainted with each other—and I am afraid this is the only sort of acquaintance I shall have the means of accomplishing between you.—And I can have no scruple on Diana's account—for her Letters shew her exactly as she is, the most active, friendly, warmhearted Being in existence, and therefore must give a good impression.'

He read.—'My dear Tom, We were all much greived at your accident, and if you had not described yourself as fallen into such very good hands, I should have been with you at all hazards the day after the receipt of your Letter, though it found me suffering under a more severe attack than usual of my old greivance, Spasmodic Bile* and hardly able to crawl from my Bed to the Sofa.—But how were you treated?—Send me more Particulars in your next.—If indeed a simple Sprain, as you denominate it, nothing would have been so judicious as Friction, Friction by the hand alone, supposing it could be applied *instantly*.—Two years ago I happened to be calling on Mrs. Sheldon when her Coachman sprained his foot as he was cleaning the Carriage and could hardly limp into the House—but by the immediate use of Friction alone, steadily persevered in, (and I rubbed his Ancle with my own hand for six Hours without Intermission)—he was well in three days.— Many Thanks my dear Tom, for the kindness with respect to us, which had so large a share in bringing on your accident.—But pray: never run into Peril again, in looking for an Apothecary on our account, for had you the most experienced Man in his Line settled at Sanditon, it would be no recommendation to us. We have entirely done with the whole Medical Tribe. We have consulted Physician after Physician in vain, till we are quite convinced that they can do nothing for us and that we must trust to our own knowledge of our own wretched Constitutions for any releif.—But if you think it advisable for the interest of the *Place*, to get a Medical Man there, I will undertake the commission with pleasure, and have no doubt of succeeding.—I could soon put the necessary Irons in the fire.—As for getting to Sanditon myself, it is quite an Impossibility. I greive to say that I dare not attempt it, but my feelings tell me too plainly that in my present state, the Sea air would probably be the death of me.—And neither of my dear Companions will leave me, or I would promote their going down to you for a fort-night. But in truth, I doubt whether Susan's nerves would be equal to the effort. She has been suffering much from the Headache, and Six Leaches* a day for ten days together releived her so little that we thought it right to change our measures—and being convinced on examination that much of the Evil lay in her Gum, I persuaded her to attack the disorder there. She has accordingly had three Teeth drawn, and is decidedly better, but her Nerves are a good deal deranged. She can only speak in a whisper—and fainted away twice this morning on poor Arthur's trying to suppress a cough. He, I am happy to say is tolerably well—tho' more languid than I like—and I fear for his Liver.—I have heard nothing of Sidney since your being together in Town, but conclude his scheme to the Isle of Wight* has not taken place, or we should have seen him in his way.

Most sincerely do we wish you a good Season at Sanditon, and though we cannot contribute to your Beau Monde* in person, we are doing our utmost to send you Company worth having; and think we may safely reckon on securing you two large Families, one a rich West Indian* from Surry, the other, a most respectable Girls Boarding School, or Academy, from Camberwell.*—I will not tell you how many People I have employed in the business—Wheel within wheel.—But Success more than repays.—Yours most affectionately—&c'

'Well'—said Mr. Parker—as he finished. 'Though I dare say Sidney might find something extremely entertaining in this Letter and make us laugh for half an hour together, I declare *I* by myself, can see nothing in it but what is either very pitiable or very credit-able.—With all their sufferings, you perceive how much they are occupied in promoting the Good of others!—So anxious for Sanditon! Two large Families—One, for Prospect House probably, the other, for No. 2. Denham Place—or the end house of the Terrace,—and extra Beds at the Hotel.—I told you my Sisters were excellent Women, Miss Heywood.'

'And I am sure they must be very extraordinary ones.'—said Charlotte. 'I am astonished at the chearful style of the Letter,

considering the state in which both Sisters appear to be.—Three
Teeth drawn at once!—frightful!—Your Sister Diana seems almost
as ill as possible, but those three Teeth of your Sister Susan's, are
more distressing than all the rest.—'

'Oh!—they are so used to the operation—to every operation—and
have such Fortitude!—'

'Your Sisters know what they are about, I dare say, but their
Measures seem to touch on Extremes.—I feel that in any illness,
I should be so anxious for Professional advice, so very little ven-
turesome for myself, or any body I loved!—But then, *we* have
been so healthy a family, that I can be no Judge of what the habit
of self-doctoring may do.—'

'Why to own the truth,' said Mrs. Parker—'I *do* think the Miss
Parkers carry it too far sometimes—and so do you my Love, you
know.—You often think they would be better, if they would leave
themselves more alone—and especially Arthur. I know you think
it a great pity they should give *him* such a turn for being ill.—'

'Well, well—my dear Mary—I grant you, it *is* unfortunate for
poor Arthur, that, at his time of Life he should be encouraged to
give way to Indisposition. It *is* bad;—it *is* bad that he should be
fancying himself too sickly for any Profession—and sit down at
one and twenty, on the interest of his own little Fortune, without
any idea of attempting to improve it, or of engaging in any occupation that may be of use to himself or others.—But let us talk of
pleasanter things.—These two large Families are just what we
wanted—But—here is something at hand, pleasanter still—Morgan,
with his "Dinner on Table."'

CHAPTER 6

THE Party were very soon moving after Dinner. Mr. Parker could not be satisfied without an early visit to the Library, and the Library Subscription book,* and Charlotte was glad to see as much, and as quickly as possible, where all was new. They were out in the very quietest part of a Watering-place Day, when the important Business of Dinner or of sitting after Dinner was going on in almost every inhabited Lodging;—here and there a solitary Elderly Man might be seen, who was forced to move early and walk for health—but in general, it was a thorough pause of Company, it was Emptiness and Tranquillity on the Terrace, the Cliffs, and the Sands.—The Shops were deserted—the Straw Hats and pendant Lace seemed left to their fate both within the House and without, and Mrs. Whitby at the Library was sitting in her inner room, reading one of her own Novels, for want of Employment.

The List of Subscribers was but commonplace. The Lady Denham, Miss Brereton, Mr. and Mrs. Parker—Sir Edward Denham and Miss Denham, whose names might be said to lead off the Season, were followed by nothing better than—Mrs. Mathews—Miss Mathews, Miss E. Mathews, Miss H. Mathews.—Dr. and Mrs. Brown—Mr. Richard Pratt.—Lieut. Smith R.N. Capt. Little,—Limehouse.—Mrs. Jane Fisher. Miss Fisher. Miss Scroggs.—Rev. Mr. Hankins. Mr. Beard—Solicitor, Grays Inn.—Mrs. Davis, and Miss Merryweather.—Mr. Parker could not but feel that the List was not only without Distinction, but less numerous than he had hoped. It was but July however, and August and September were the Months;—And besides, the promised large Families from Surry and Camberwell, were an ever-ready consolation.

Mrs. Whitby came forward without delay from her Literary recess, delighted to see Mr. Parker again, whose manners recommended him to every body, and they were fully occupied in their various Civilities and Communications, while Charlotte having

added her name to the List as the first offering to the success of the
Season, was busy in some immediate purchases for the further good
of Everybody, as soon as Miss Whitby could be hurried down from
her Toilette, with all her glossy Curls and smart Trinkets, to wait on
her.—The Library of course, afforded every thing; all the useless
things in the World that could not be done without, and among so
many pretty Temptations, and with so much good will for Mr.
Parker to encourage Expenditure, Charlotte began to feel that she
must check herself—or rather she reflected that at two and Twenty
there could be no excuse for her doing otherwise—and that it would
not do for her to be spending all her Money the very first Evening.
She took up a Book; it happened to be a volume of *Camilla*.* She
had not *Camilla's* Youth, and had no intention of having her
Distress,—so, she turned from the Drawers of rings and Broches
repressed farther solicitation and paid for what she bought.

For her particular gratification, they were then to take a Turn on
the Cliff—but as they quitted the Library they were met by two
Ladies whose arrival made an alteration necessary, Lady Denham
and Miss Brereton.—They had been to Trafalgar House, and
been directed thence to the Library, and though Lady Denham
was a great deal too active to regard the walk of a mile as any thing
requiring rest, and talked of going home again directly, the Parkers
knew that to be pressed into their House, and obliged to take her
Tea with them, would suit her best,—and therefore the stroll on
the Cliff gave way to an immediate return home.

'No, no,' said her Ladyship—'I will not have you hurry your
Tea on my account.—I know you like your Tea late.—My early
hours are not to put my Neighbours to inconvenience. No, no,
Miss Clara and I will get back to our own Tea.—We came out with
no other Thought.—We wanted just to see you and make sure of
your being really come—, but we get back to our own Tea.'

She went on however towards Trafalgar House and took possession of the Drawing room very quietly—without seeming to hear
a word of Mrs. Parker's orders to the Servant as they entered, to
bring Tea directly.

Charlotte was fully consoled for the loss of her walk, by finding
herself in company with those, whom the conversation of the

morning had given her a great curiosity to see. She observed them well.—Lady Denham was of middle height, stout, upright and alert in her motions, with a shrewd eye, and self-satisfied air—but not an unagreable Countenance—and tho' her manner was rather downright and abrupt, as of a person who valued herself on being free-spoken, there was a good humour and cordiality about her—a civility and readiness to be acquainted with Charlotte herself, and a heartiness of welcome towards her old friends, which was inspiring the Good will she seemed to feel;—And as for Miss Brereton, her appearance so completely justified Mr. Parker's praise that Charlotte thought she had never beheld a more lovely, or more Interesting young Woman.—Elegantly tall, regularly handsome, with great delicacy of complexion and soft Blue eyes, a sweetly modest and yet naturally Graceful Address, Charlotte could see in her only the most perfect representation of whatever Heroine might be most beautiful and bewitching, in all the numerous volumes they had left behind them on Mrs. Whitby's shelves.

Perhaps it might be partly oweing to her having just issued from a Circulating Library—but she could not separate the idea of a complete Heroine from Clara Brereton. Her situation with Lady Denham so very much in favour of it!—She seemed placed with her on purpose to be ill-used. Such Poverty and Dependance joined to such Beauty and Merit, seemed to leave no choice in the business.—These feelings were not the result of any spirit of Romance in Charlotte herself. No, she was a very sober-minded young Lady, sufficiently well-read in Novels to supply her Imagination with amusement, but not at all unreasonably influenced by them; and while she pleased herself the first five minutes with fancying the Persecutions which *ought* to be the Lot of the interesting Clara, especially in the form of the most barbarous conduct on Lady Denham's side, she found no reluctance to admit from subsequent observation, that they appeared to be on very comfortable Terms.—She could see nothing worse in Lady Denham, than the sort of oldfashioned formality of always calling her *Miss Clara*—nor anything objectionable in the degree of observance and attention which Clara paid.—On one side it seemed protecting kindness, on the other grateful and affectionate respect.

The Conversation turned entirely upon Sanditon, its present number of Visitants, and the Chances of a good Season. It was evident that Lady Denham had more anxiety, more fears of loss, than her Coadjutor. She wanted to have the Place fill faster, and seemed to have many harassing apprehensions of the Lodgings being in some instances underlet.—Miss Diana Parker's two large Families were not forgotten.

'Very good, very good,' said her Ladyship.—'A West Indy Family and a school. That sounds well. That will bring Money.'

'No people spend more freely, I beleive, than West Indians.' observed Mr. Parker.

'Aye—so I have heard—and because they have full Purses, fancy themselves equal, may be, to your old Country Families. But then, they who scatter their Money so freely, never think of whether they may not be doing mischeif by raising the price of Things—And I have heard that's very much the case with your West-injines—and if they come among us to raise the price of our necessaries of Life, we shall not much thank them Mr. Parker.'

'My dear Madam, They can only raise the price of consumeable Articles, by such an extraordinary Demand for them and such a diffusion of Money among us, as must do us more Good than harm.—Our Butchers and Bakers and Traders in general cannot get rich without bringing Prosperity to *us*.—If *they* do not gain, our rents must be insecure—and in proportion to their profit must be ours eventually in the increased value of our Houses.'

'Oh!—well.—But I should not like to have Butcher's meat raised, though—and I shall keep it down as long as I can.—Aye—that young Lady smiles I see;—I dare say she thinks me an odd sort of a Creature,—but *she* will come to care about such matters herself in time. Yes, Yes, my Dear, depend upon it, you will be thinking of the price of Butcher's meat in time—though you may not happen to have quite such a Servants Hall full to feed, as I have.—And I do beleive *those* are best off, that have fewest Servants.—I am not a Woman of Parade, as all the World knows, and if it was not for what I owe to poor Mr. Hollis's memory, I should never keep up Sanditon House as I do;—it is not for my own pleasure.—Well Mr. Parker—and the other is a Boarding school, a French Boarding

School,* is it?—No harm in that.—They'll stay their six weeks.—
And out of such a number, who knows but some may be consump-
tive and want Asses milk*—and I have two Milch asses at this
present time.—But perhaps the little Misses may hurt the
Furniture.—I hope they will have a good sharp Governess to
look after them.—'

Poor Mr. Parker got no more credit from Lady Denham than he
had from his Sisters, for the object which had taken him to
Willingden.

'Lord! my dear Sir,' she cried, 'how could you think of such
a thing? I am very sorry you met with your accident, but upon my
word you deserved it.—Going after a Doctor!—Why, what should
we do with a Doctor here? It would be only encouraging our
Servants and the Poor to fancy themselves ill, if there was a Doctor
at hand.—Oh! pray, let us have none of the Tribe at Sanditon. We
go on very well as we are. There is the Sea and the Downs and
my Milch-Asses—and I have told Mrs. Whitby that if any body
enquires for a Chamber-Horse,* they may be supplied at a fair
rate—(poor Mr. Hollis's Chamber-Horse, as good as new)—and
what can People want for, more?—Here have I lived seventy good
years in the world and never took Physic above twice—and never
saw the face of a Doctor in all my Life, on my *own* account.—And
I verily beleive if my poor dear Sir Harry had never seen one neither, he would have been alive now.—Ten fees, one after another,
did the Man take who sent *him* out of the World.—I beseech you
Mr. Parker, no Doctors here.'—

The Tea things were brought in.—'Oh! my dear Mrs. Parker—you
should not indeed—why would you do so? I was just upon the
point of wishing you good Evening. But since you are so very
neighbourly, I beleive Miss Clara and I must stay.'

CHAPTER 7

THE popularity of the Parkers brought them some visitors the very next morning;—amongst them, Sir Edward Denham and his Sister, who having been at Sanditon House drove on to pay their Compliments; and the duty of Letter-writing being accomplished, Charlotte was settled with Mrs. Parker—in the Drawing room in time to see them all.—The Denhams were the only ones to excite particular attention. Charlotte was glad to complete her knowledge of the family by an introduction to them, and found them, the better half at least—(for while single, the *Gentleman* may sometimes be thought the better half, of the pair)—not unworthy notice.—Miss Denham was a fine young woman, but cold and reserved, giving the idea of one who felt her consequence with Pride and her Poverty with Discontent, and who was immediately gnawed by the want of an handsomer Equipage than the simple Gig in which they travelled, and which their Groom was leading about still in her sight.—Sir Edward was much her superior in air and manner;—certainly handsome, but yet more to be remarked for his very good address and wish of paying attention and giving pleasure.—He came into the room remarkably well, talked much—and very much to Charlotte, by whom he chanced to be placed—and she soon perceived that he had a fine Countenance, a most pleasing gentleness of voice, and a great deal of Conversation. She liked him.—Sober-minded as she was, she thought him agreable, and did not quarrel with the suspicion of his finding her equally so, which *would* arise from his evidently disregarding his Sister's motion to go, and persisting in his station and his discourse.

I make no apologies for my Heroine's vanity.—If there are young Ladies in the World at her time of Life, more dull of Fancy and more careless of pleasing, I know them not, and never wish to know them.

At last, from the low French windows of the Drawing room which commanded the road and all the Paths across the Down, Charlotte and Sir Edward as they sat, could not but observe Lady

Denham and Miss Brereton walking by—and there was instantly
a slight change in Sir Edward's countenance—with an anxious
glance after them as they proceeded—followed by an early pro-
posal to his Sister—not merely for moving, but for walking on
together to the Terrace—which altogether gave an hasty turn to
Charlotte's fancy, cured her of her halfhour's fever, and placed her
in a more capable state of judging, when Sir Edward was gone, of
how agreable he had actually been.—'Perhaps there was a good
deal in his Air and Address; And his Title did him no harm.'

She was very soon in his company again. The first object of the
Parkers, when their House was cleared of morning visitors was to
get out themselves;—the Terrace was the attraction to all;—Every
body who walked, must begin with the Terrace, and there, seated
on one of the two Green Benches by the Gravel walk, they found
the united Denham Party;—but though united in the Gross, very
distinctly divided again—the two superior Ladies being at one
end of the bench, and Sir Edward and Miss Brereton at the other.

Charlotte's first glances told her that Sir Edward's air was that
of a Lover.—There could be no doubt of his Devotion to Clara.—How
Clara received it, was less obvious—but she was inclined to think
not very favourably; for tho' sitting thus apart with him (which
probably she might not have been able to prevent) her Air was calm
and grave.—That the young Lady at the other end of the Bench
was doing Penance, was indubitable. The difference in Miss
Denham's countenance, the change from Miss Denham sitting in
cold Grandeur in Mrs. Parker's Drawing-room to be kept from
silence by the efforts of others, to Miss Denham at Lady Denham's
Elbow, listening and talking with smiling attention or solicitous
eagerness, was very striking—and very amusing—or very melancholy, just as Satire or Morality might prevail.—Miss Denham's
Character was pretty well decided with Charlotte.

Sir Edward's required longer Observation. He surprised her by
quitting Clara immediately on their all joining and agreeing to
walk, and by addressing his attentions entirely to herself.—Stationing
himself close by her, he seemed to mean to detach her as much as
possible from the rest of the Party and to give her the whole of his
Conversation. He began, in a tone of great Taste and Feeling, to

talk of the Sea and the Sea shore—and ran with Energy through all the usual Phrases employed in praise of their Sublimity, and descriptive of the *undescribable* Emotions they excite in the Mind of Sensibility.—The terrific Grandeur of the Ocean in a Storm, its glassy surface in a calm, its Gulls and its Samphire, and the deep fathoms of its Abysses, its quick vicissitudes, its direful Deceptions, its Mariners tempting it in Sunshine and over-whelmed by the sudden Tempest, All were eagerly and fluently touched;—rather commonplace perhaps—but doing very well from the Lips of a handsome Sir Edward,—and she could not but think him a Man of Feeling*—till he began to stagger her by the number of his Quotations, and the bewilderment of some of his sentences.

'Do you remember,' said he, 'Scott's beautiful Lines on the Sea?—Oh! what a description they convey!—They are never out of my Thoughts when I walk here.—That Man who can read them unmoved must have the nerves of an Assassin!—Heaven defend me from meeting such a Man un-armed.'

'What description do you mean?'—said Charlotte. 'I remember none at this moment, of the Sea, in either of Scott's Poems.'*

'Do not you indeed?—Nor can I exactly recall the beginning at this moment—But—you cannot have forgotten his description of Woman.—

> "Oh! Woman in our Hours of Ease—"

Delicious! Delicious!—Had he written nothing more, he would have been Immortal. And then again, that unequalled, unrivalled Address to Parental affection—

> "Some feelings are to Mortals given
> With less of Earth in them than Heaven" &c

But while we are on the subject of Poetry, what think you Miss Heywood of Burns Lines to his Mary?*—Oh! there is Pathos to madden one!—If ever there was a Man who *felt*, it was Burns.—Montgomery has all the Fire of Poetry, Wordsworth has the true soul of it—Campbell* in his Pleasures of Hope has touched the extreme of our Sensations—"Like Angel's visits, few and far between." Can you conceive any thing more subduing, more melting, more fraught with the deep Sublime than that Line?—But Burns—I confess my sense of his Pre-eminence Miss Heywood—If Scott *has* a fault, it is the want of Passion.—Tender, Elegant, Descriptive—but *Tame*.—The Man who cannot do justice to the attributes of Woman is my contempt.—Sometimes indeed a flash of feeling seems to irradiate him—as in the Lines we were speaking of—"Oh! Woman in our hours of Ease"—. But Burns is always on fire.—His Soul was the Altar in which lovely Woman sat enshrined, his Spirit truly breathed the immortal Incence which is her Due.—'

'I have read several of Burns' Poems with great delight,' said Charlotte as soon as she had time to speak, 'but I am not poetic enough to separate a Man's Poetry entirely from his Character;—and poor Burns's known Irregularities, greatly interrupt my enjoyment of his Lines.—I have difficulty in depending on the *Truth* of his Feelings as a Lover. I have not faith in the *sincerity* of the affections of a Man of his Description. He felt and he wrote and he forgot.'

'Oh! no no'—exclaimed Sir Edward in an extasy. 'He was all ardour and Truth!—His Genius and his Susceptibilities might lead him into some Aberrations—But who is perfect?—It were Hyper-criticism, it were Pseudo-philosophy to expect from the soul of high toned Genius, the grovellings of a common mind.— The Coruscations of Talent, elicited by impassioned feeling in the breast of Man, are perhaps incompatible with some of the prosaic Decencies of Life;—nor can you, loveliest Miss Heywood (speaking with an air of deep sentiment)—nor can any Woman be a fair Judge of what a Man may be propelled to say, write or do, by the sovereign impulses of illimitable Ardour.'

This was very fine;—but if Charlotte understood it at all, not very moral—and being moreover by no means pleased with his extraordinary stile of compliment, she gravely answered 'I really know nothing of the matter.—This is a charming day. The Wind I fancy must be Southerly.'

'Happy, happy Wind, to engage Miss Heywood's Thoughts!—' She began to think him downright silly.—His chusing to walk with her, she had learnt to understand. It was done to pique Miss

Brereton. She had read it, in an anxious glance or two on his side—but why he should talk so much Nonsense, unless he could do no better, was un-intelligible.—He seemed very sentimental, very full of some Feelings or other, and very much addicted to all the newest-fashioned hard words—had not a very clear Brain she presumed, and talked a good deal by rote.—The Future might explain him further—but when there was a proposition for going into the Library she felt that she had had quite enough of Sir Edward for one morning, and very gladly accepted Lady Denham's invitation of remaining on the Terrace with her.

The others all left them, Sir Edward with looks of very gallant despair in tearing himself away, and they united their agreable-ness—that is, Lady Denham like a true great Lady, talked and talked only of her own concerns, and Charlotte listened—amused in considering the contrast between her two companions.—Certainly, there was no strain of doubtful Sentiment, nor any phrase of diffi-cult interpretation in Lady Denham's discourse. Taking hold of Charlotte's arm with the ease of one who felt that any notice from her was an Honour, and communicative, from the influence of the same conscious Importance or a natural love of talking, she imme-diately said in a tone of great satisfaction—and with a look of arch sagacity—'Miss Esther wants me to invite her and her Brother to spend a week with me at Sanditon House, as I did last Summer—but I shan't.—She has been trying to get round me every way, with her praise of this, and her praise of that; but I saw what she was about.—I saw through it all.—I am not very easily taken-in my Dear.'

Charlotte could think of nothing more harmless to be said, than the simple enquiry of—'Sir Edward and Miss Denham?'

'Yes, my Dear. *My young Folks*, as I call them sometimes, for I take them very much by the hand. I had them with me last Summer, about this time, for a week; from Monday to Monday; and very delighted and thankful they were.—For they are very good young People my Dear. I would not have you think that I *only* notice them, for poor dear Sir Harry's sake. No, no; they are very deserving them-selves, or trust me, they would not be so much in *my* Company.—I am not the Woman to help any body blindfold.—I always take care to know what I am about and who I have to deal with, before I stir

a finger.—I do not think I was ever over-reached in my Life; and
That is a good deal for a woman to say that has been married
twice.—Poor dear Sir Harry (between ourselves) thought at first
to have got more.—But (with a bit of a sigh) He is gone, and we
must not find fault with the Dead. Nobody could live happier
together than us—and he was a very honourable Man, quite the
Gentleman of ancient Family.—And when he died, I gave Sir
Edward his Gold Watch.—'

She said this with a look at her Companion which implied its
right to produce a great Impression—and seeing no rapturous
astonishment in Charlotte's countenance, added quickly—

'He did not bequeath it to his Nephew, my dear—It was no
bequest. It was not in the Will. He only told me, and *that* but once,
that he should wish his Nephew to have his Watch; but it need not
have been binding, if I had not chose it.—'

'Very kind indeed! very Handsome!'—said Charlotte, absolutely forced to affect admiration.

'Yes, my dear—and it is not the *only* kind thing I have done by
him.—I have been a very liberal friend to Sir Edward. And poor
young Man, he needs it bad enough;—For though I am *only* the
Dowager my Dear, and he is the *Heir*, things do not stand between
us in the way they commonly do between those two parties.—Not
a shilling do I receive from the Denham Estate. Sir Edward has no
Payments to make *me*. He don't stand uppermost, beleive me.—It
is *I* that help *him*.'

'Indeed!—He is a very fine young Man;—particularly Elegant
in his Address.'—This was said cheifly for the sake of saying
something—but Charlotte directly saw that it was laying her open
to suspicion by Lady Denham's giving a shrewd glance at her and
replying—

'Yes, yes, he is very well to look at—and it is to be hoped some
Lady of large fortune will think so—for Sir Edward *must* marry for
Money.—He and I often talk that matter over.—A handsome
young fellow like him, will go smirking and smiling about and
paying girls Compliments, but he knows he *must* marry for
Money.—And Sir Edward is a very steady young Man in the
main, and has got very good notions.'

'Sir Edward Denham,' said Charlotte, 'with such personal Advantages may be almost sure of getting a Woman of fortune, if he chuses it.'

This glorious sentiment seemed quite to remove suspicion.

'Aye my Dear—That's very sensibly said' cried Lady Denham. 'And if we could but get a young Heiress to Sanditon! But Heiresses are monstrous scarce! I do not think we have had an Heiress here, or even a Co-* since Sanditon has been a public place. Families come after Families, but as far as I can learn, it is not one in an hundred of them that have any real Property, Landed or Funded.*—An Income perhaps, but no Property. Clergymen may be, or Lawyers from Town, or Half pay officers,* or Widows with only a Jointure.* And what good can such people do anybody?—except just as they take our empty Houses—and (between ourselves) I think they are great fools for not staying at home. Now, if we could get a young Heiress to be sent here for her health—(and if she was ordered to drink asses milk I could supply her)—and as soon as she got well, have her fall in love with Sir Edward!'

'That would be very fortunate indeed.'

'And Miss Esther must marry somebody of fortune too—She must get a rich Husband. Ah! young Ladies that have no Money are very much to be pitied!—But'—after a short pause—'if Miss Esther thinks to talk me into inviting them to come and stay at Sanditon House, she will find herself mistaken.—Matters are altered with me since last Summer you know—. I have Miss Clara with me now, which makes a great difference.'

She spoke this so seriously that Charlotte instantly saw in it the evidence of real penetration and prepared for some fuller remarks—but it was followed only by—'I have no fancy for having my House as full as an Hotel. I should not chuse to have my two Housemaids Time taken up all the morning, in dusting out Bed rooms.—They have Miss Clara's room to put to rights as well as my own every day.—If they had hard Places, they would want Higher Wages.—'

For objections of this Nature, Charlotte was not prepared, and she found it so impossible even to affect simpathy, that she could say nothing.

Lady Denham soon added, with great glee—'And besides all this my Dear, am I to be filling my House to the prejudice of Sanditon?—If People want to be by the Sea, why dont they take Lodgings?—Here are a great many empty Houses—three on this very Terrace; no fewer than three Lodging Papers staring us in the face at this very moment, Numbers 3, 4 and 8. Eight, the Corner House may be too large for them, but either of the two others are nice little snug Houses, very fit for a young Gentleman and his Sister—And so, my dear, the next time Miss Esther begins talking about the dampness of Denham Park, and the Good Bathing always does her, I shall advise them to come and take one of these Lodgings for a fortnight.—Don't you think that will be very fair?—Charity begins at home you know.'

Charlotte's feelings were divided between amusement and indignation—but indignation had the larger and the increasing share.—She kept her Countenance and she kept a civil Silence. She could not carry her forbearance farther; but without attempting to listen longer, and only conscious that Lady Denham was still talking on in the same way, allowed her Thoughts to form themselves into such a Meditation as this.—'She is thoroughly mean. I had not expected any thing so bad.—Mr. Parker spoke too mildly of her.—His Judgement is evidently not to be trusted.—His own Goodnature misleads him. He is too kind hearted to see clearly.—I must judge for myself.—And their very *connection* prejudices him.—He has persuaded her to engage in the same Speculation—and because their object in that Line is the same, he fancies she feels like him in others.—But she is very, very mean.—I can see no Good in her.—Poor Miss Brereton!—And she makes every body mean about her.—This poor Sir Edward and his Sister,—how far Nature meant them to be respectable I cannot tell,—but they are *obliged* to be Mean in their Servility to her.—And I am Mean too, in giving her my attention, with the appearance of coinciding with her.—Thus it is, when Rich People are Sordid.'

CHAPTER 8

THE two Ladies continued walking together till rejoined by the others, who as they issued from the Library were followed by a young Whitby running off with five volumes under his arm to Sir Edward's Gig—and Sir Edward approaching Charlotte, said 'You may perceive what has been our occupation. My Sister wanted my Counsel in the selection of some books.—We have many leisure hours, and read a great deal.—I am no indiscriminate Novel-Reader. The mere Trash of the common Circulating Library, I hold in the highest contempt. You will never hear me advocating those puerile Emanations which detail nothing but discordant Principles incapable of Amalgamation, or those vapid tissues of ordinary occurrences from which no useful Deductions can be drawn.—In vain may we put them into a literary Alembic;*—we distil nothing which can add to Science.—You understand me I am sure?'

'I am not quite certain that I do.—But if you will describe the sort of Novels which you *do* approve, I dare say it will give me a clearer idea.'

'Most willingly, Fair Questioner.—The Novels which I approve are such as display Human Nature with Grandeur—such as shew her in the Sublimities of intense Feeling—such as exhibit the progress of strong Passion from the first Germ of incipient Susceptibility to the utmost Energies of Reason half-dethroned,—where we see the strong spark of Woman's Captivations elicit such Fire in the Soul of Man as leads him—(though at the risk of some Aberration from the strict line of Primitive Obligations)—hazard all, dare all, atcheive all, to obtain her.—Such are the Works which I peruse with delight, and I hope I may say, with Amelioration. They hold forth the most splendid Portraitures of high Conceptions, Unbounded Veiws, illimitable ardour, indomptible Decision—and even when the Event is mainly anti-prosperous to the high-toned Machinations of the prime Character, the potent, pervading Hero of the Story, it leaves us full of Generous Emotions for him;—our

Hearts are paralized—. T'were Pseudo-Philosophy to assert that we do not feel more enwraped by the brilliancy of his Career, than by the tranquil and morbid Virtues of any opposing Character. Our approbation of the Latter is but Eleemosynary.—These are the Novels which enlarge the primitive Capabilities of the Heart, and which it cannot impugn the Sense or be any Dereliction of the character, of the most anti-puerile* Man, to be conversant with.'

'If I understand you aright'—said Charlotte—'our taste in Novels is not at all the same.' And here they were obliged to part—Miss Denham being too much tired of them all, to stay any longer.

The truth was that Sir Edward whom Circumstances had confined very much to one spot had read more sentimental Novels than agreed with him. His fancy had been early caught by all the impassioned, and most exceptionable parts of Richardsons; and such Authors as have since appeared to tread in Richardson's steps, so far as Man's determined pursuit of Woman in defiance of every opposition of feeling and convenience is concerned, had since occupied the greater part of his literary hours, and formed his Character.—With a perversity of Judgement, which must be attributed to his not having by Nature a very strong head, the Graces, the Spirit, the Ingenuity, and the Perseverance, of the Villain of the Story outweighed all his absurdities and all his Atrocities with Sir Edward. With him, such Conduct was Genius, Fire and Feeling.—It interested and inflamed him; and he was always more anxious for its Success and mourned over its Discomfitures with more Tenderness than could ever have been contemplated by the Authors.—Though he owed many of his ideas to this sort of reading, it were unjust to say that he read nothing else, or that his Language were not formed on a more general knowledge of modern Literature.—He read all the Essays, Letters, Tours and Criticisms of the day—and with the same ill-luck which made him derive only false Principles from Lessons of Morality, and incentives to Vice from the History of its Overthrow, he gathered only hard words and involved sentences from the style of our most approved Writers.

Sir Edward's great object in life was to be seductive.—With such personal advantages as he knew himself to possess, and such

Talents as he did also give himself credit for, he regarded it as his Duty.—He felt that he was formed to be a dangerous Man—quite in the line of the Lovelaces.*—The very name of Sir Edward, he thought, carried some degree of fascination with it.—To be generally gallant and assiduous about the fair, to make fine speeches to every pretty Girl, was but the inferior part of the Character he had to play.—Miss Heywood, or any other young Woman with any pretensions to Beauty, he was entitled (according to his own veiws of Society) to approach with high Compliments and Rhapsody on the slightest acquaintance; but it was Clara alone on whom he had serious designs; it was Clara whom he meant to seduce.—Her seduction was quite determined on. Her Situation in every way called for it. She was his rival in Lady Denham's favour, she was young, lovely and dependant.—He had very early seen the necessity of the case, and had now been long trying with cautious assiduity to make an impression on her heart, and to undermine her Principles.

Clara saw through him, and had not the least intention of being seduced—but she bore with him patiently enough to confirm the sort of attachment which her personal Charms had raised.—A greater degree of discouragement indeed would not have affected Sir Edward—. He was armed against the highest pitch of Disdain or Aversion.—If she could not be won by affection, he must carry her off. He knew his Business.—Already had he had many Musings on the Subject. If he *were* constrained so to act, he must naturally wish to strike out something new, to exceed those who had gone before him—and he felt a strong curiosity to ascertain whether the Neighbourhood of Tombuctoo* might not afford some solitary House adapted for Clara's reception,—but the Expence alas! of Measures in that masterly style was ill-suited to his Purse, and Prudence obliged him to prefer the quietest sort of ruin and disgrace for the object of his Affections, to the more renowned.

CHAPTER 9

ONE day, soon after Charlotte's arrival at Sanditon, she had the pleasure of seeing just as she ascended from the Sands to the Terrace, a Gentleman's Carriage with Post Horses* standing at the door of the Hotel, as very lately arrived, and by the quantity of Luggage taking off, bringing, it might be hoped, some respectable family determined on a long residence.

Delighted to have such good news for Mr. and Mrs. Parker, who had both gone home some time before, she proceeded for Trafalgar House with as much alacrity as could remain, after having been contending for the last two hours with a very fine wind blowing directly on shore; but she had not reached the little Lawn, when she saw a Lady walking nimbly behind her at no great distance; and convinced that it could be no acquaintance of her own, she resolved to hurry on and get into the House if possible before her. But the Stranger's pace did not allow this to be accomplished;—Charlotte was on the Steps and had rung, but the door was not opened, when the other crossed the Lawn;—and when the Servant appeared, they were just equally ready for entering the House.

The ease of the Lady, her 'How do you do Morgan?—' and Morgan's Looks on seeing her, were a moment's astonishment—but another moment brought Mr. Parker into the Hall to welcome the Sister he had seen from the Drawing room, and she was soon introduced to Miss Diana Parker.

There was a great deal of surprise but still more pleasure in seeing her.—Nothing could be kinder than her reception from both Husband and Wife. 'How did she come? and with whom?—And they were so glad to find her equal to the Journey!—And that she was to belong to *them*, was a thing of course.'

Miss Diana Parker was about four and thirty, of middling height and slender;—delicate looking rather than sickly; with an agreable face, and a very animated eye;—her manners resembling her Brother's in their ease and frankness, though with more decision and less mildness in her Tone. She began an account of herself without delay.—Thanking them for their Invitation, but '*that* was quite out of the question, for they were all three come, and meant to get into Lodgings and make some stay.'

'All three come!—What!—Susan and Arthur!—Susan able to come too!—This was better and better.'

'Yes—We are actually all come. Quite unavoidable—Nothing else to be done.—You shall hear all about it.—But my dear Mary, send for the Children;—I long to see them.'

'And how has Susan born the Journey?—and how is Arthur?—and why do not we see him here with you?'

'Susan has born it wonderfully. She had not a wink of sleep either the night before we set out, or last night at Chichester, and as this is not so common with her as with *me*, I have had a thousand fears for her—but she had kept up wonderfully.—had no Hysterics of consequence till we came within sight of poor old Sanditon—and the attack was not very violent—nearly over by the time we reached your Hotel—so that we got her out of the Carriage extremely well, with only Mr. Woodcock's assistance—and when I left her she was directing the Disposal of the Luggage, and helping old Sam uncord the Trunks.—She desired her best Love, with a thousand regrets at being so poor a Creature that she could not come with me. And as for poor Arthur, he would not have been unwilling himself, but there is so much Wind that I did not think he could safely venture,—for I am *sure* there is Lumbago hanging about him—and so I helped him on with his great Coat and sent him off to the Terrace, to take us Lodgings.—Miss Heywood must have seen our Carriage standing at the Hotel.—I knew Miss Heywood the moment I saw her before me on the Down.—My dear Tom I am glad to see you walk so well. Let me feel your Ancle.—That's right; all right and clean. The play of your Sinews a *very* little affected:—barely perceptible.—Well—now for the explanation of my being here.—I told you in my Letter, of the two considerable Families, I was hoping to secure for you—the West Indians, and the Seminary.*—'

Here Mr. Parker drew his Chair still nearer to his Sister, and took her hand again most affectionately as he answered 'Yes, Yes;—How active and how kind you have been!'

'The West-indians,' she continued, 'whom I look upon as the *most* desirable of the two—as the Best of the Good—prove to be a Mrs. Griffiths and her family. I know them only through others.—You must have heard me mention Miss Capper, the particular friend of *my* very particular friend Fanny Noyce;—now, Miss Capper is extremely intimate with a Mrs. Darling, who is on terms of constant correspondence with Mrs. Griffiths herself.—Only a *short* chain, you see, between us, and not a Link wanting. Mrs. Griffiths meant to go to the Sea, for her young People's benefit—had fixed on the coast of Sussex, but was undecided as to the where, wanted something Private, and wrote to ask the opinion of her friend Mrs. Darling.—Miss Capper happened to be staying with Mrs. Darling when Mrs. Griffiths's Letter arrived, and was consulted on the question; *she* wrote the same day to Fanny Noyce and mentioned it to her—and Fanny all alive for *us*, instantly took up her pen and forwarded the circumstance to me—except as to *Names*—which have but lately transpired.—There was but *one* thing for *me* to do.—I answered Fanny's Letter by the same Post and pressed for the recommendation of Sanditon. Fanny had feared your having no house large enough to receive such a Family.—But I seem to be spinning out my story to an endless length.—You see how it was all managed. I had the pleasure of hearing soon afterwards by the same simple link of connection that Sanditon *had been* recommended by Mrs. Darling, and that the West-indians were very much disposed to go thither.—This was the state of the case when I wrote to you;—but two days ago;—yes, the day before yesterday—I heard again from Fanny Noyce, saying that *she* had heard from Miss Capper, who by a Letter from Mrs. Darling understood that Mrs. Griffiths—has expressed herself in a letter to Mrs. Darling more doubtingly on the subject of Sanditon.—Am I clear? I would be anything rather than not clear.'

'Oh! perfectly, perfectly. Well?'

'The reason of this hesitation, was her having no connections in the place, and no means of ascertaining that she should have good accommodations on arriving there;—and she was particularly careful and scrupulous on all those matters more on account of a certain Miss Lambe a young Lady (probably a Neice) under her care, than on her own account or her Daughters.—Miss Lambe

has an immense fortune—richer than all the rest—and very deli-
cate health.—One sees clearly enough by all this, the *sort* of
Woman Mrs. Griffiths must be—as helpless and indolent, as
Wealth and a Hot Climate are apt to make us. But we are not all
born to equal Energy.—What was to be done?—I had a few
moments indecision;—Whether to offer to write to *you*,—or to
Mrs. Whitby to secure them a House?—but neither pleased me.—
I hate to employ others, when I am equal to act myself—and my
conscience told me that this was an occasion which called for me.
Here was a family of helpless Invalides whom I might essentially
serve.—I sounded Susan—the same Thought had occurred to
her.—Arthur made no difficulties—our plan was arranged immediately, we were off yesterday morning at six—, left Chichester at
the same hour today—and here we are.—'

'Excellent—Excellent!—' cried Mr. Parker.—'Diana, you are
unequalled in serving your friends and doing Good to all the
World.—I know nobody like you.—Mary, my Love, is not she
a wonderful Creature?—Well—and now, what House do you
design to engage for them?—What is the size of their family?—'

'I do not at all know'—replied his Sister—'have not the least
idea;—never heard any particulars;—but I am very sure that the
largest house at Sanditon cannot be *too* large. They are more likely
to want a second.—I shall take only one however, and that, but for
a week certain.—Miss Heywood, I astonish you.—You hardly
know what to make of me.—I see by your Looks, that you are not
used to such quick measures.'

The words 'Unaccountable Officiousness!—Activity run mad!'—
had just passed through Charlotte's mind—but a civil answer was
easy. 'I dare say I do look surprised,' said she—'because these are
very great exertions, and I know what Invalides both you and your
Sister are.'

'Invalides indeed.—I trust there are not three People in England
who have so sad a right to that appellation!—But my dear Miss
Heywood, we are sent into this World to be as extensively useful as
possible, and where some degree of Strength of Mind is given, it
is not a feeble body which will excuse us—or incline us to excuse
ourselves.—The World is pretty much divided between the Weak

of Mind and the Strong—between those who can act and those who can not, and it is the bounden Duty of the Capable to let no opportunity of being useful escape them.—My Sister's Complaints and mine are happily not often of a nature, to threaten Existence *immediately*—and as long as we *can* exert ourselves to be of use to others, I am convinced that the Body is the better, for the refreshment the Mind receives in doing its Duty.—While I have been travelling, with this object in veiw, I have been perfectly well.'

The entrance of the Children ended this little panegyric on her own Disposition—and after having noticed and caressed them all,—she prepared to go.

'Cannot you dine with us?—Is not it possible to prevail on you to dine with us?' was then the cry; and *that* being absolutely negatived, it was 'And when shall we see you again? and how can we be of use to you?'—and Mr. Parker warmly offered his assistance in taking the house for Mrs. Griffiths—

'I will come to you the moment I have dined,' said he, 'and we will go about together.'

But this was immediately declined.—'No, my dear Tom, upon no account in the World, shall you stir a step on any business of mine.—Your Ancle wants rest. I see by the position of your foot, that you have used it too much already.—No, I shall go about my House-taking directly. Our Dinner is not ordered till six—and by that time I hope to have completed it. It is now only half past four.—As to seeing *me* again today—I cannot answer for it; the others will be at the Hotel all the Evening, and delighted to see you at any time, but as soon as I get back I shall hear what Arthur has done about our own Lodgings, and probably the moment Dinner is over, shall be out again on business relative to them, for we hope to get into some Lodgings or other and be settled after breakfast tomorrow.—I have not much confidence in poor Arthur's skill for Lodging-taking, but he seemed to like the commission.—'

'I think you are doing too much,' said Mr. Parker. 'You will knock yourself up. You should not move again after Dinner.'

'No, indeed you should not,' cried his wife, 'for Dinner is such a mere *name* with you all, that it can do you no good.—I know what your appetites are.—'

'My appetite is very much mended I assure you lately. I have been taking some Bitters of my own decocting, which have done wonders. Susan never eats I grant you—and just at present *I* shall want nothing; I never eat for about a week after a Journey—but as for Arthur, he is only too much disposed for Food. We are often obliged to check him.'

'But you have not told me any thing of the *other* Family coming to Sanditon,' said Mr. Parker as he walked with her to the door of the House—'the Camberwell Seminary; have we a good chance of *them*?'

'Oh! Certain—quite certain.—I had forgotten them for the moment, but I had a letter three days ago from my friend Mrs. Charles Dupuis which assured me of Camberwell. Camberwell will be here to a certainty, and very soon.—*That* good Woman (I do not know her name) not being so wealthy and independant as Mrs. Griffiths—can travel and chuse for herself.—I will tell you how I got at *her*. Mrs. Charles Dupuis lives almost next door to a Lady, who has a relation lately settled at Clapham, who actually attends the Seminary and gives lessons on Eloquence and Belles Lettres to some of the Girls.—I got that Man a Hare from one of Sidney's friends—and he recommended Sanditon;—Without *my* appearing however—Mrs. Charles Dupuis managed it all.—'

CHAPTER 10

IT was not a week, since Miss Diana Parker had been told by her feelings, that the Sea Air would probably in her present state, be the death of her, and now she was at Sanditon, intending to make some Stay, and without appearing to have the slightest recollection of having written or felt any such thing.—It was impossible for Charlotte not to suspect a good deal of fancy in such an extraordinary state of health.—Disorders and Recoveries so very much out of the common way, seemed more like the amusement of eager minds in want of employment than of actual afflictions and releif. The Parkers, were no doubt a family of Imagination and quick feelings—and while the eldest Brother found vent for his superfluity of sensation as a Projector,* the Sisters were perhaps driven to dissipate theirs in the invention of odd complaints.—The *whole* of their mental vivacity was evidently not so employed; Part was laid out in a Zeal for being useful.—It should seem that they must either be very busy for the Good of others, or else extremely ill themselves. Some natural delicacy of Constitution in fact, with an unfortunate turn for medecine, especially quack Medecine, had given them an early tendency at various times, to various Disorders;—the rest of their Sufferings was from Fancy, the love of Distinction and the love of the Wonderful.—They had Charitable hearts and many amiable feelings—but a spirit of restless activity, and the glory of doing more than anybody else, had their share in every exertion of Benevolence—and there was Vanity in all they did, as well as in all they endured.

Mr. and Mrs. Parker spent a great part of the Evening at the Hotel; but Charlotte had only two or three veiws of Miss Diana posting over the Down after a House for this Lady whom she had never seen, and who had never employed her.

She was not made acquainted with the others till the following day, when, being removed into Lodgings and all the party continuing quite well, their Brother and Sister and herself were entreated to drink tea with them.—They were in one of the Terrace

Houses—and she found them arranged for the Evening in a small neat Drawing room, with a beautiful veiw of the Sea if they had chosen it,—but though it had been a very fair English Summer-day,—not only was there no open window, but the Sopha and the Table, and the Establishment in general was all at the other end of the room by a brisk fire.

Miss Parker whom, remembering the three Teeth drawn in one day, Charlotte approached with a peculiar degree of respectful Compassion, was not very unlike her Sister in person or man-ner—tho' more thin and worn by Illness and Medecine, more relaxed in air, and more subdued in voice. She talked however, the whole Evening, as incessantly as Diana—and excepting that she sat with salts in her hand, took Drops two or three times from one, out of the several Phials already at home on the Mantlepeice,—and made a great many odd faces and contortions, Charlotte could perceive no symptoms of illness which she, in the boldness of her own good health, would not have undertaken to cure, by putting out the fire, opening the Window, and disposing of the Drops and the Salts by means of one or the other.

She had had considerable curiosity to see Mr. Arthur Parker; and having fancied him a very puny, delicate-looking young Man, the smallest very materially of not a robust Family, was astonished to find him quite as tall as his Brother and a great deal Stouter—Broad made and Lusty*—and with no other look of an Invalide, than a sodden complexion.—Diana was evidently the cheif of the fam-ily; principal Mover and Actor;—she had been on her Feet the whole Morning, on Mrs. Griffiths's business or their own, and was still the most alert of the three.—Susan had only superintended their final removal from the Hotel, bringing two heavy Boxes her-self, and Arthur had found the air so cold that he had merely walked from one House to the other, as nimbly as he could,—and boasted much of sitting by the fire till he had cooked up a very good one.

Diana, whose exercise had been too domestic to admit of calcu-lation, but who, by her own account, had not once sat down during the space of seven hours, confessed herself a little tired. She had been too successful however for much fatigue; for not only had she by walking and talking down a thousand difficulties at last secured a proper House at eight Guineas per week for Mrs. Griffiths; she had also opened so many Treaties with Cooks, Housemaids, Washer-women and Bathing Women, that Mrs. Griffiths would have little more to do on her arrival, than to wave her hand and collect them around her for Choice.—Her concluding effort in the cause, had been a few polite lines of Information to Mrs. Griffiths herself—time not allowing for the circuitous train of intelligence which had been hitherto kept up,—and she was now regaling in the delight of opening the first Trenches of an acquaintance with such a powerful discharge of unexpected Obligation.

Mr. and Mrs. Parker and Charlotte had seen two Post chaises crossing the Down to the Hotel as they were setting off,—a joyful sight—and full of speculation.—The Miss Parkers—and Arthur had also seen something;—they could distinguish from their window that there *was* an arrival at the Hotel, but not its amount. Their visitors answered for two Hack-Chaises.*—Could it be the Camberwell Seminary?—No.—No.—Had there been a third carriage, perhaps it might; but it was very generally agreed that two Hack chaises could never contain a Seminary.—Mr. Parker was confident of another new Family.—

When they were all finally seated, after some removals to look at the Sea and the Hotel, Charlotte's place was by Arthur, who was sitting next to the Fire with a degree of Enjoyment which gave a good deal of merit to his civility in wishing her to take his Chair.—There was nothing dubious in her manner of declining it, and he sat down again with much satisfaction. She drew back her Chair to have all the advantage of his Person as a screen, and was very thankful for every inch of Back and Shoulders beyond her pre-conceived idea.

Arthur was heavy in Eye as well as figure, but by no means indisposed to talk;—and while the other four were cheifly engaged together, he evidently felt it no penance to have a fine young Woman next to him, requiring in common Politeness some attention—as his Brother, who felt the decided want of some motive for action, some Powerful object of animation for him, observed with considerable pleasure.—Such was the influence of Youth and

Bloom that he began even to make a sort of apology for having a Fire. 'We should not have one at home,' said he, 'but the Sea air is always damp. I am not afraid of any thing so much as Damp.—'

'I am so fortunate,' said Charlotte, 'as never to know whether the air is damp or dry. It has always some property that is wholesome and invigorating to me.—'

'*I* like the Air too, as well as any body can;' replied Arthur, 'I am very fond of standing at an open window when there is no Wind—but unluckily a Damp air does not like *me*.—It gives me the Rheumatism.—You are not rheumatic I suppose?—'

'Not at all.'

'That's a great blessing.—But perhaps you are nervous.'

'No—I beleive not. I have no idea that I am.—'

'*I* am very nervous.—To say the truth Nerves are the worst part of my Complaints in *my* opinion. My Sisters think me Bilious, but I doubt it.—'

'You are quite in the right, to doubt it as long as you possibly can, I am sure.—'

'If I were Bilious,' he continued, 'you know Wine would disagree with me, but it always does me good.—The more Wine I drink (in moderation) the better I am.—I am always best of an Evening.—If you had seen me to day before Dinner, you would have thought me a very poor creature.—'

Charlotte could beleive it—. She kept her countenance however, and said—'As far as I can understand what nervous complaints are, I have a great idea of the efficacy of Air and exercise for them:—daily, regular Exercise;—and I should recommend rather more of it to *you* than I suspect you are in the habit of taking.'

'Oh! I am very fond of exercise myself'—he replied—'and mean to walk a great deal while I am here, if the Weather is temperate. I shall be out every morning before breakfast and take several turns upon the Terrace, and you will often see me at Trafalgar House.'

'But you do not call a walk to Trafalgar House much exercise?—'

'Not, as to mere distance, but the Hill is so steep!—Walking up that Hill, in the middle of the day, would throw me into such a Perspiration!—You would see me all in a Bath, by the time I got there!—I am very subject to Perspiration, and there cannot be a surer sign of Nervousness.—'

They were now advancing so deep in Physics,* that Charlotte veiwed the entrance of the Servant with the Tea things, as a very fortunate Interruption.—It produced a great and immediate change. The young Man's attentions were instantly lost. He took his own Cocoa from the Tray,—which seemed provided with almost as many Teapots &c as there were persons in company, Miss Parker drinking one sort of Herb-Tea and Miss Diana another, and turning completely to the Fire, sat coddling and cooking it to his own satisfaction and toasting some Slices of Bread, brought up ready-prepared in the Toast rack—and till it was all done, she heard nothing of his voice but the murmuring of a few broken sentences of self-approbation and success.—When his Toils were over however, he moved back his Chair into as gallant a Line as ever, and proved that he had not been working only for himself, by his earnest invitation to her to take both Cocoa and Toast.—She was already helped to Tea—which surprised him—so totally self-engrossed had he been.

'I thought I should have been in time,' said he, 'but Cocoa takes a great deal of Boiling.'

'I am much obliged to you,' replied Charlotte—'but I *prefer* Tea.'

'Then I will help myself,' said he.—'A large Dish of rather weak Cocoa every evening agrees with me better than any thing.'

It struck her however, as he poured out this rather weak Cocoa, that it came forth in a very fine, dark coloured Stream—and at the same moment, his Sisters both crying out—'Oh! Arthur, you get your Cocoa stronger and stronger every Evening'—, with Arthur's somewhat conscious reply of '*Tis* rather stronger than it should be tonight'—convinced her that Arthur was by no means so fond of being starved as they could desire, or as he felt proper himself.—He was certainly very happy to turn the conversation on dry Toast, and hear no more of his sisters.

'I hope you will eat some of this Toast,' said he, 'I reckon myself a very good Toaster; I never burn my Toasts—I never put them too near the Fire at first—and yet, you see, there is not a Corner but what is well browned.—I hope you like dry Toast.'

'With a reasonable quantity of Butter spread over it, very much'—said Charlotte—'but not otherwise.—'

'No more do I'—said he exceedingly pleased—'We think quite alike there.—So far from dry Toast being wholesome, *I* think it a very bad thing for the Stomach. Without a little butter to soften it, it hurts the Coats of the Stomach.* I am sure it does.—I will have the pleasure of spreading some for you directly—and afterwards I will spread some for myself.—Very bad indeed for the Coats of the Stomach—but there is no convincing *some* people.—It irritates and acts like a nutmeg grater.—'

He could not get the command of the Butter however, without a struggle; His Sisters accusing him of eating a great deal too much, and declaring he was not to be trusted;—and he maintaining that he only eat enough to secure the Coats of his Stomach;—and besides, he only wanted it now for Miss Heywood.—Such a plea must prevail, he got the butter and spread away for her with an accuracy of Judgement which at least delighted himself; but when her Toast was done, and he took his own in hand, Charlotte could hardly contain herself as she saw him watching his Sisters, while he scrupulously scraped off almost as much butter as he put on, and then seize an odd moment for adding a great dab just before it went into his Mouth.—Certainly, Mr. Arthur Parker's enjoyments in Invalidism were very different from his Sisters— by no means so spiritualized.—A good deal of Earthy Dross hung about him. Charlotte could not but suspect him of adopting that line of Life, principally for the indulgence of an indolent Temper—and to be determined on having no Disorders but such as called for warm rooms and good Nourishment.—In one particular however, she soon found that he had caught something from *them*.

'What!' said he—'Do you venture upon two dishes of strong Green Tea in one Evening?—What Nerves you must have!—How I envy you.—Now, if *I* were to swallow only one such dish—what do you think it's effect would be upon me?—'

'Keep you awake perhaps all night'—replied Charlotte, meaning to overthrow his attempts at Surprise, by the Grandeur of her own Conceptions.

'Oh! if that were all!'—he exclaimed.—'No—it acts on me like Poison and would entirely take away the use of my right side, before I had swallowed it five minutes.—It sounds almost incredible—but it has happened to me so often that I cannot doubt it.—The use of my right Side is entirely taken away for several hours!'

'It sounds rather odd to be sure'—answered Charlotte coolly—'but I dare say it would be proved to be the simplest thing in the World, by those who have studied right sides and Green Tea scientifically and thoroughly understand all the possibilities of their action on each other.'

Soon after Tea, a Letter was brought to Miss Diana Parker from the Hotel.—'From Mrs. Charles Dupuis'—said she.—'some private hand.'—And having read a few lines, exclaimed aloud 'Well, this is very extraordinary! very extraordinary indeed!—That both should have the same name.—Two Mrs. Griffiths!—This is a Letter of recommendation and introduction to me, of the Lady from Camberwell—and *her* name happens to be Griffiths too.—' A few lines more however, and the colour rushed into her Cheeks, and with much Perturbation she added—'The oddest thing that ever was!—a Miss Lambe too!—a young Westindian of large Fortune.—But it *cannot* be the same.—Impossible that it should be the same.'

She read the Letter aloud for comfort.—It was merely to 'introduce the Bearer, Mrs. Griffiths—from Camberwell, and the three young Ladies under her care, to Miss Diana Parker's notice.—Mrs. Griffiths—being a stranger at Sanditon, was anxious for a respectable Introduction—and Mrs. Charles Dupuis therefore, at the instance of the intermediate friend, provided her with this Letter, knowing that she could not do her dear Diana a greater kindness than by giving her the means of being useful.—Mrs. Griffiths's cheif solicitude would be for the accomodation and comfort of one of the young Ladies under her care, a Miss Lambe, a young West Indian of large Fortune, in delicate health.'

'It was very strange!—very remarkable!—very extraordinary' but they were all agreed in determining it to be *impossible* that there should not be two Families; such a totally distinct set of people as were concerned in the reports of each, made that matter quite certain. There *must* be two Families.—Impossible to be otherwise. 'Impossible' and 'Impossible', was repeated over and over again with great fervour.—An accidental resemblance of Names and circumstances, however striking at first, involved nothing really incredible—and so it was settled.

Miss Diana herself derived an immediate advantage to counterbalance her Perplexity. She must put her shawl over her shoulders, and be running about again. Tired as she was, she must instantly repair to the Hotel, to investigate the truth and offer her Services.

CHAPTER 11

IT would not do.—Not all that the whole Parker race could say among themselves, could produce a happier catastrophé than that the Family from Surry and the Family from Camberwell were one and the same.—The rich Westindians, and the young Ladies Seminary had all entered Sanditon in those two Hack chaises. The Mrs. Griffiths who in her friend Mrs. Darling's hands, had wavered as to coming and been unequal to the Journey, was the very same Mrs. Griffiths whose plans were at the same period (under another representation) perfectly decided, and who was without fears or difficulties.—All that had the appearance of Incongruity in the reports of the two, might very fairly be placed to the account of the Vanity, the Ignorance, or the blunders of the many engaged in the cause by the vigilance and caution of Miss Diana Parker. *Her* intimate friends must be officious like herself, and the subject had supplied Letters and Extracts and Messages enough to make everything appear what it was not.

Miss Diana probably felt a little awkward on being first obliged to admit her mistake. A long Journey from Hampshire taken for nothing—a Brother disappointed—an expensive House on her hands for a week, must have been some of her immediate reflections—and much worse than all the rest, must have been the sort of sensation of being less clear-sighted and infallible than she had beleived herself.—No part of it however seemed to trouble her long. There were so many to share in the shame and the blame, that probably when she had divided out their proper portions to Mrs. Darling, Miss Capper, Fanny Noyce, Mrs. Charles Dupuis and Mrs. Charles Dupuis's Neighbour, there might be a mere trifle of reproach remaining for herself.—At any rate, she was seen all the following morning walking about after Lodgings with Mrs. Griffiths—as alert as ever.

Mrs. Griffiths was a very well-behaved, genteel kind of Woman, who supported herself by receiving such great girls and young Ladies, as wanted either Masters for finishing their Education, or a home for beginning their Displays—She had several more under her care than the three who were now come to Sanditon, but the others all happened to be absent.

Of these three, and indeed of all, Miss Lambe was beyond comparison the most important and precious, as she paid in proportion to her fortune.—She was about seventeen, half-mulatto,* chilly and tender, had a maid of her own, was to have the best room in the Lodgings, and was always of the first consequence in every plan of Mrs. Griffiths.

The other Girls, two Miss Beauforts were just such young Ladies as may be met with, in at least one family out of three, throughout the Kingdom; they had tolerable complexions, shewey figures, an upright decided carriage and an assured Look;—they were very accomplished and very Ignorant, their time being divided between such pursuits as might attract admiration, and those Labours and Expedients of dexterous Ingenuity, by which they could dress in a stile much beyond what they *ought* to have afforded; they were some of the first in every change of fashion—and the object of all, was to captivate some Man of much better fortune than their own.

Mrs. Griffiths had preferred a small, retired place, like Sanditon, on Miss Lambe's account—and the Miss Beauforts, though naturally preferring any thing to Smallness and Retirement, yet having in the course of the Spring been involved in the inevitable expense of six new Dresses each for a three days visit, were constrained to be satisfied with Sanditon also, till their circumstances were retrieved. There, with the hire of a Harp for one, and the purchase of some Drawing paper for the other and all the finery they could already command, they meant to be very economical, very elegant and very secluded; with the hope on Miss Beaufort's side, of praise and celebrity from all who walked within the sound of her Instrument, and on Miss Letitia's, of curiosity and rapture in all who came near her while she sketched—and to Both, the consolation of meaning to be the most stylish Girls in the Place.

The particular introduction of Mrs. Griffiths to Miss Diana Parker, secured them immediately an acquaintance with the Trafalgar House-family, and with the Denhams;—and the Miss Beauforts were soon satisfied with 'the Circle in which they moved in Sanditon' to use a proper phrase, for every body must now 'move in a Circle',—to the prevalence of which rotatory motion, is perhaps to be attributed the Giddiness and false steps of many.

Lady Denham had other motives for calling on Mrs. Griffiths besides attention to the Parkers.—In Miss Lambe, here was the very young Lady, sickly and rich, whom she had been asking for; and she made the acquaintance for Sir Edward's sake, and the sake of her Milch asses. How it might answer with regard to the Baronet, remained to be proved, but as to the Animals, she soon found that all her calculations of Profit would be vain. Mrs. Griffiths would not allow Miss Lambe to have the smallest symptom of a Decline, or any complaint which Asses milk could possibly releive. 'Miss Lambe was under the constant care of an experienced Physician;—and his Prescriptions must be their rule'—and except in favour of some Tonic Pills,* which a Cousin of her own had a Property in, Mrs. Griffiths did never deviate from the strict medecinal page.

The corner house of the Terrace was the one in which Miss Diana Parker had the pleasure of settling her new friends, and considering that it commanded in front the favourite Lounge of all the Visitors at Sanditon, and on one side, whatever might be going on at the Hotel, there could not have been a more favourable spot for the seclusions of the Miss Beauforts. And accordingly, long before they had suited themselves with an Instrument, or with Drawing paper, they had, by the frequency of their appearance at the low Windows upstairs, in order to close the blinds, or open the Blinds, to arrange a flower pot on the Balcony, or look at nothing through a Telescope, attracted many an eye upwards, and made many a Gazer gaze again.

A little novelty has a great effect in so small a place; the Miss Beauforts, who would have been nothing at Brighton, could not move here without notice;—and even Mr. Arthur Parker, though little disposed for supernumerary exertion, always quitted the Terrace, in his way to his Brothers by this corner House, for the sake of a glimpse of the Miss Beauforts, though it was half a quarter of a mile round about, and added two steps to the ascent of the Hill.

CHAPTER 12

CHARLOTTE had been ten days at Sanditon without seeing Sanditon House, every attempt at calling on Lady Denham having been defeated by meeting with her beforehand. But now it was to be more resolutely undertaken, at a more early hour, that nothing might be neglected of attention to Lady Denham or amusement to Charlotte.

'And if you should find a favourable opening my Love,' said Mr. Parker (who did not mean to go with them)—'I think you had better mention the poor Mullins's situation, and sound her Ladyship as to a Subscription for them. I am not fond of charitable subscriptions in a place of this kind—It is a sort of tax upon all that come—Yet as their distress is very great and I almost promised the poor Woman yesterday to get something done for her, I beleive we must set a subscription on foot—and therefore the sooner the better,—and Lady Denham's name at the head of the List will be a very necessary beginning.—You will not dislike speaking to her about it, Mary?'

'I will do whatever you wish me,' replied his wife—'but you would do it so much better yourself. I shall not know what to say.'

'My dear Mary,' cried he, 'it is impossible you can be really at a loss. Nothing can be more simple. You have only to state the present afflicted situation of the family, their earnest application to me, and my being willing to promote a little subscription for their releif, provided it meet with her approbation.—'

'The easiest thing in the World'—cried Miss Diana Parker who happened to be calling on them at the moment—. 'All said and done, in less time than you have been talking of it now.—And while you are on the subject of subscriptions Mary, I will thank you to mention a very melancholy case to Lady Denham, which has been represented to me in the most affecting terms.—There is a poor Woman in Worcestershire, whom some friends of mine are exceedingly interested about, and I have undertaken to collect whatever I can for her. If you would mention the circumstance to Lady

Denham!—Lady Denham *can* give, if she is properly attacked—and I look upon her to be the sort of Person who, when once she is prevailed on to undraw her Purse, would as readily give ten Guineas as five.—And therefore, if you find her in a Giving mood, you might as well speak in favour of another Charity which I and a few more, have very much at heart—the establishment of a Charitable Repository* at Burton on Trent.—And then,—there is the family of the poor Man who was hung last assizes at York, tho' we really *have* raised the sum we wanted for putting them all out, yet if you *can* get a Guinea from her on their behalf, it may as well be done.—'

'My dear Diana!' exclaimed Mrs. Parker—'I could no more mention these things to Lady Denham—than I could fly.'

'Where's the difficulty?—I wish I could go with you myself—but in five minutes I must be at Mrs. Griffiths—to encourage Miss Lambe in taking her first Dip. She is so frightened, poor Thing, that I promised to come and keep up her Spirits, and go in the Machine with her if she wished it—and as soon as that is over, I must hurry home, for Susan is to have Leaches at one o'clock—which will be a three hours business,—therefore I really have not a moment to spare—besides that (between ourselves) I ought to be in bed myself at this present time, for I am hardly able to stand—and when the Leaches have done, I dare say we shall both go to our rooms for the rest of the day.'

'I am sorry to hear it, indeed; but if this is the case I hope Arthur will come to us.'

'If Arthur takes my advice, he will go to bed too, for if he stays up by himself, he will certainly eat and drink more than he ought;—but you see Mary, how impossible it is for me to go with you to Lady Denham's.'

'Upon second thoughts Mary,' said her husband, 'I will not trouble you to speak about the Mullins's.—I will take an opportunity of seeing Lady Denham myself.—*I* know how little it suits you to be pressing matters upon a Mind at all unwilling.'

His application thus withdrawn, his Sister could say no more in support of hers, which was his object, as he felt all their impropriety and all the certainty of their ill effect upon his own better claim.

Mrs. Parker was delighted at this release, and set off very happy with her friend and her little girl, on this walk to Sanditon House.—It was a close, misty morning, and when they reached the brow of the Hill, they could not for some time make out what sort of Carriage it was, which they saw coming up. It appeared at different moments to be everything from the Gig to the Pheaton,— from one horse to four; and just as they were concluding in favour of a Tandem,* little Mary's young eyes distinguished the Coachman and she eagerly called out, 'T''is Uncle Sidney Mama, it is indeed.'

And so it proved.—Mr. Sidney Parker driving his Servant in a very neat Carriage was soon opposite to them; and they all stopped for a few minutes. The manners of the Parkers were always pleasant among themselves—and it was a very friendly meeting between Sidney and his sister-in-law, who was most kindly taking it for granted that he was on his way to Trafalgar House. This he declined however. 'He was just come from Eastbourne, proposing to spend two or three days, as it might happen, at Sanditon—but the Hotel must be his Quarters—He was expecting to be joined there by a friend or two.'—The rest was common enquiries and remarks, with kind notice of little Mary, and a very well-bred Bow and proper address to Miss Heywood on her being named to him—and they parted, to meet again within a few hours.

Sidney Parker was about seven or eight and twenty, very good-looking, with a decided air of Ease and Fashion, and a lively countenance.

This adventure afforded agreable discussion for some time. Mrs. Parker entered into all her Husband's joy on the occasion, and exulted in the credit which Sidney's arrival would give to the place.

The road to Sanditon House was a broad, handsome, planted approach, between fields, and conducting at the end of a quarter of a mile through second Gates into the Grounds, which though not extensive had all the Beauty and Respectability which an abundance of very fine Timber could give.—These Entrance Gates were so much in a corner of the Grounds or Paddock, so near one of its Boundaries, that an outside fence was at first almost

pressing on the road—till an angle *here*, and a curve there threw
them to a better distance. The Fence was a proper, Park paling* in
excellent condition; with clusters of fine Elms, or rows of old
Thorns following its line almost every where.—*Almost* must be
stipulated—for there were vacant spaces—and through one of
these, Charlotte as soon as they entered the Enclosure, caught
a glimpse over the pales of something White and Womanish in the
field on the other side;—it was a something which immediately
brought Miss Brereton into her head—and stepping to the pales,
she saw indeed—and very decidedly, in spite of the Mist; Miss
Brereton—seated, not far before her, at the foot of the bank which
sloped down from the outside of the Paling and which a narrow
Path seemed to skirt along;—Miss Brereton seated, apparently
very composedly—and Sir Edward Denham by her side.—They
were sitting so near each other and appeared so closely engaged in
gentle conversation, that Charlotte instantly felt she had nothing
to do but to step back again, and say not a word.—Privacy was
certainly their object.—It could not but strike her rather unfavour-
ably with regard to Clara;—but hers was a situation which must
not be judged with severity.—She was glad to perceive that nothing had been discerned by Mrs Parker; If Charlotte had not been
considerably the tallest of the two, Miss Brereton's white ribbons
might not have fallen within the ken of *her* more observant
eyes.—Among other points of moralising reflection which the
sight of this Tete a Tete produced, Charlotte could not but think
of the extreme difficulty which secret Lovers must have in finding
a proper spot for their stolen Interveiws.—Here perhaps they had
thought themselves so perfectly secure from observation—the
whole field open before them—a steep bank and Pales never crossed
by the foot of Man at their back—and a great thickness of air, in
aid—. Yet here she had seen them. They were really ill-used.

The House was large and handsome; two Servants appeared,
to admit them, and every thing had a suitable air of Property
and Order.—Lady Denham valued herself upon her liberal
Establishment, and had great enjoyment in the order and the
Importance of her style of living.—They were shewn into the
usual sitting room, well-proportioned and well-furnished;—tho'

it was Furniture rather originally good and extremely well kept, than new or shewey—and as Lady Denham was not there, Charlotte had leisure to look about, and to be told by Mrs. Parker that the whole-length Portrait of a stately Gentleman, which placed over the Mantlepeice, caught the eye immediately, was the picture of Sir Harry Denham—and that one among many miniatures in another part of the room, little conspicuous, represented Mr. Hollis.—Poor Mr. Hollis!—It was impossible not to feel him hardly used; to be obliged to stand back in his own House and see the best place by the fire constantly occupied by Sir Harry Denham.

EXPLANATORY NOTES

In these notes, references to Jane Austen's novels follow the practice of modern editions and cite continuous chapter numbers, not volume and chapter number.

JA is used as an abbreviation for Jane Austen.

OED is *The Oxford English Dictionary*, 2nd edn, 20 vols (Oxford: Oxford University Press, 1989), with revisions in the online edition up to 2018.

3 *Tunbridge . . . Hastings . . . East-Bourne*: in the opening pages JA takes great care to locate her imaginary characters, Mr and Mrs Parker, and later the rival fictional seaside resorts of Sanditon and Brinshore, within precise and real geographic co-ordinates. Tunbridge is JA's spelling for Tonbridge in Kent, 29 miles south-east of London. Willingden, where the Parkers' coach overturns, is a real place (Willingdon) about two miles inland from Eastbourne on the Sussex coast. Great Willingden and Willingden Abbots are fictional. Seaside resorts were springing up all along England's extensive southern coastline from the later eighteenth century. Brighton (originally 'Brighthelmston(e)') was the first, developed in the 1750s and 1760s. As one early nineteenth-century guidebook observed: 'In process of time, should the present taste continue, it is not improbable but that every paltry village on the Sussex coast which has a convenient beach for bathing will rise to a considerable town' (*A Guide to all the Watering and Sea-Bathing Places* (London, 1803), 202). Other locations mentioned are Battel (JA's spelling for 'Battle'), eight miles from Hastings, and Hailsham, ten miles north of Eastbourne, both inland towns in East Sussex. Worthing is a seaside resort ten miles west of Brighton (Eastbourne is about twenty miles east of Brighton), and the Weald stretches between the chalk uplands of the North and South Downs. Sanditon is placed at the foot of the South Downs in East Sussex.

4 *Surgeon*: also styled 'surgeon apothecary', a general practitioner who dispensed medicines and treated a range of surgical and physical conditions. As yet, it was a relatively low-status profession. At p. 28, Diana Parker uses 'apothecary' to cover the same profession.

5 *Morning Post . . . Kentish Gazette*: actual newspapers of the time. The *Morning Post*, a London daily newspaper, began publication in 1772; the *Kentish Gazette* was a twice-weekly local paper published in Canterbury from 1768 and covering the area of East Sussex in which the imaginary town of Sanditon is located.

Post-chaises: the most expensive form of hired transport, usually four-wheeled closed carriages whose horses were changed at regular 'posts' (inns or post-houses) to maximize speed.

6 *Turnpike road*: one on which a toll or fee was collected to maintain it in good repair.

6 *Saline air and immersion*: the growth in English seaside resorts fuelled a spate of books and pamphlets extolling the health benefits of sea air, sea bathing, and sea-water baths (buildings to which sea water was pumped): Dr Richard Russell, *A Dissertation on the Use of Sea-Water in the Diseases of the Glands* (in Latin, 1750; English version 1752); A. P. Buchan, *Practical Observations concerning Sea Bathing* (1804); William Nisbet, *A Medical Guide for the Invalid to the Principal Watering Places of Great Britain; containing a view of the medicinal effects of water, etc.* (1804); John Gibney, *Practical Observations on the Use and Abuse of Cold and Warm Sea-Bathing, in various diseases* (1813). Hot and cold sea baths were constructed at Brighton in 1759; a sea-bathing infirmary opened at Margate in 1796 and a sea-water bath at Worthing in 1798.

7 *Nursery Grounds*: 'an area of land used for raising young plants' (*OED*).

8 *two or three speculating People*: people gambling on quick or high returns for their investments. As here, an economic term, 'speculation' was morally loaded at the time, carrying a suggestion of irresponsibility. Adam Smith, the great eighteenth-century economist, described the 'speculative merchant' as one who 'exercises no one regular, established, or well-known branch of business . . . He enters into every trade when he foresees that it is likely to be more than commonly profitable, and he quits it when he foresees that its profits are likely to return to the level of other trades. . . . A bold adventurer may sometimes acquire a considerable fortune by two or three successful speculations; but is just as likely to lose one by two or three unsuccessful ones' (*An Inquiry into the Nature and Causes of the Wealth of Nations*, 2 vols (London, 1776), i. 140 (Book 1, ch. 10)). Speculation of various kinds is set to be a major theme in the novel (see Introduction, pp. xiv–xv). The association with gaming was reinforced by the contemporary card game of Speculation, which involved 'the buying and selling of trump cards, the holder of the highest trump card in a round winning the pool' (*OED*). The game is played in JA's third published novel, *Mansfield Park* (1814), ch. 25, and we know that she enjoyed it herself (see *Letters*, 170–1 (10–11 January 1809)).

effluvia: disgusting smells (here of seaweed) thought to be harmful to health.

that line of the Poet Cowper: William Cowper (1731–1800). The quotation is from 'Truth', line 334, in *Poems* (London, 1782), 89–90, and contrasts a happy peasant, content with her faith, with the famous philosopher Voltaire, pseudonym of François-Marie Arouet (1694–1778), imagined as unhappy because of his scepticism:

> Just knows, and knows no more, her Bible true—
> A truth the brilliant Frenchman never knew;
> . . . .
> O happy peasant! O unhappy Bard!
> His the mere tinsel, hers the rich reward;
> He prais'd perhaps for ages yet to come;
> She never heard of half a mile from home.

Its application here, where Brinshore is likened to the happy peasant, wrenches the passage a considerable way from its original meaning.

11 *Enthusiast*: applied (from the seventeenth century) to religious zealots, the term carried both positive and negative connotations. In his *Dictionary* (1755), Samuel Johnson offers the primary definition as 'One who vainly imagines a private revelation'. Mr Parker is clearly a passionate advocate for Sanditon, with an early hint that he may also be obsessively self-deluded.

12 *collateral Inheritance*: an inheritance from a childless relative.

his Mine . . . Lottery . . . Speculation . . . Hobby Horse: all examples to show Mr Parker as a fantasist willing to risk his 'easy though not large fortune' (p. 11) in unlikely money-making ventures or speculations. As Adam Smith noted: 'That the chance of gain is naturally overvalued, we may learn from the universal success of lotteries . . . There is not . . . a more certain proposition in mathematicks than that the more tickets you adventure upon, the more likely you are to be a loser' (*An Inquiry into . . . the Wealth of Nations*, i. 132 (Book 1, ch. 10)). State lotteries had flourished since 1694 and ran almost uninterrupted to 1826. They were viewed as a legitimate method of raising funds for ventures in the public interest—in London, the building of the British Museum and construction of Westminster Bridge. But from the 1770s, when cash prizes could be as high as £20,000, their use was more widespread and open to abuse. Several private lotteries were authorized by Parliament at this time. In JA's teenage story 'Edgar & Emma', Mr Willmot owns a share in a lead mine and has bought a ticket in the state lottery (*Teenage Writings*, ed. Kathryn Sutherland and Freya Johnston (Oxford: Oxford University Press, 2017), 25). A hobby horse (originally a child's toy consisting of a long stick with a horse's head at one end) is something pursued out of all proportion.

13 *anti-spasmodic . . . anti-rheumatic*: JA makes fun of the medical jargon of the time with its obscure coinages. George Motherby, *A New Medical Dictionary* (3rd edn, 1791), 89 ff., includes many terms with the prefix '*anti*' (against): '*antiarthritica*, medicines against the gout'; '*antifebrile*, remedies against a fever'; '*antispasmodicum*, a remedy against convulsions'. Later, in Chapters 7 and 8, Sir Edward Denham's absurd literary jargon satirizes his critical pretentions. Here and elsewhere in *Sanditon*, JA is not beyond coining a few bizarre words of her own, like 'anti-sceptic' (presumably for 'antiseptic').

14 *Library*: an important social venue in every spa and seaside resort. As well as loaning books, the library would be expected to stock trinkets to tempt holidaymakers, to sell tickets for local entertainments, and perhaps to hire out musical instruments. At Bognor Regis on the Sussex coast, still a modest resort in 1815, 'the proprietor has diversified his library with an assortment of fancy articles, jewelry, music, prints . . . so that this may be justly said, to be the only place of resort for those who seek to vary the tranquil pleasures of retirement, by the recreation of a library' (*A Guide to all the Watering and Sea-Bathing Places* (London, 1815), 147). In JA's second novel,

Lydia Bennet saw in the library at Brighton 'such beautiful ornaments as made her quite wild' (*Pride and Prejudice* (1813), ch. 42).

14 *five shillings*: in JA's manuscript, it was originally 'one night' rather than 'five shillings' (roughly equivalent to £25 today) that Mr Heywood promised not to spend at Brinshore.

17 *Coadjutor*: helper in a project or task.

Cottage Ornèe: (JA uses 'è' rather than the expected 'é'); a mock-rustic retreat for wealthy holidaymakers wishing to play at simple country living. The cottage ornée, fashionable from the later eighteenth century, was designed for both picturesque effect and modern convenience. See John Plaw, *Ferme Ornée; or, rural improvements . . . calculated for landscape and picturesque effects* (1800); and *Rural Residences, consisting of a series of designs for cottages, decorated cottages, small villas, and other ornamental buildings* (1818).

Michaelmas: 29 September, the feast day of St Michael and one of the four 'quarter days' of the year, when regular legal and financial transactions took place.

21 *Trafalgar House . . . Waterloo Crescent*: the enthusiasm for naming buildings after national wartime victories was nothing new. *Sanditon* is set in the immediate aftermath of Britain's long wars against Revolutionary and Napoleonic France. The Battle of Trafalgar, 21 October 1805, saw Admiral Nelson's victory over the French fleet; the Battle of Waterloo, 18 June 1815, marked Napoleon's final defeat. The Strand Bridge, in London, begun in 1811, was renamed Waterloo Bridge in 1816. Terraces of houses constructed in the shape of a crescent were relatively new. The name was first used for the Royal Crescent at Bath, built 1767–75 (*OED*). Brighton's Royal Crescent, 1798–1807, was the first to be built facing the sea. Crescents were associated with luxurious accommodation. These topical points of reference all show Mr Parker's determination to be up to date. For him, events that happened a little more than ten years earlier already seem like the distant past.

23 *equipage*: this might refer simply to Sidney Parker's generally fashionable appearance or 'get up', or more widely to his carriage, horses, and attendant servants. Either way, an equipage was a clear indication of social status.

24 *Blue Shoes . . . nankin Boots*: blue shoes were fashionable for women from the 1790s; but the reference may be more specific—to the bright blue known as 'Waterloo blue': 'The most fashionable colours are—cinnamon, brown, Waterloo-blue, and different shades of green' (1815, *British Lady's Magazine*, quoted in *OED*). For a qualification, see Elizabeth Smith (Grant), *Memoirs of a Highland Lady*, ed. Andrew Tod, 2 vols (Edinburgh: Canongate Classics, 1988), ii. 35, describing events in 1815–16: 'We were inundated this whole winter with a deluge of a dull ugly colour called Waterloo bleu, copied from the dye used in Flanders for the calico of which the peasantry make their smock frocks or blouses. Everything new was Waterloo, not unreasonably, it has been such a victory, such an event,

after so many years of exhausting suffering. And as a surname to hats, coats, trowsers, instruments, furniture, it was very well—a very fair way of trying to perpetuate the return of tranquillity; but to deluge us with that vile indigo, so unbecoming even to the fairest! It was really a punishment . . . that Waterloo [blue] was really an affliction, none of us were sufficiently patriotick to deform ourselves by trying it.'

Nankin or nankeen is 'a kind of pale yellowish cloth, originally made at Nanking' in China (*OED*); the material was hard-wearing and could be used for the uppers of ladies' boots; subsequently, the term also meant the colour of nankin, 'pale yellow, or buff' (*OED*, sense 1a and 1c).

25 *Bathing Machines*: huts on wheels with a door at either end, they were drawn by horse into the sea. The bather stripped inside the hut and entered the water with the assistance of a helper of their own sex. Different fashions were observed in different resorts. At Bognor, on the Sussex coast, there were in 1815 'ten or twelve machines . . . which are drawn to any depth required: at low water the bathers may go even as far out as the rocks. The ladies will find a female guide, but there is no awning to the machines, as is customary on the Kentish, and some other coast' (*A Guide to all the Watering and Sea Bathing Places*, 149). Since nude bathing was recommended as most beneficial, the Bognor machines clearly offered less protection for female modesty.

venetian window: a window with three separate openings, the two side ones being narrow. A recent innovation, the design let in more light and air than traditional smaller, leaded panes. *OED* notes a first use in English in 1775.

28 *Spasmodic Bile*: bile is the bitter fluid produced by the liver. Excessive production by or obstruction of the bile ducts would cause bouts of nausea and pain. In her final illness JA suffered bilious attacks and became 'more & more convinced that <u>Bile</u> is at the bottom of all I have suffered' (*Letters*, 341 (24 January 1817)).

29 *Leaches*: blood-sucking worms, leeches were specifically bred for and widely used in a variety of medical purposes.

Isle of Wight: a small island off the south coast of England and already a popular tourist destination in the eighteenth century.

Beau Monde: already a rather clichéd term for fashionable society.

West Indian: not natives of the West Indies but a European family made wealthy by investment or trade there. In *Mansfield Park* (ch. 3), Sir Thomas Bertram has an 'estate', presumably a sugar plantation, in the West Indies. As the responses of the Sanditon gentry indicate, West Indian families were envied and courted for their riches but they might also be considered inferior to the best society and tainted by association with slavery.

Camberwell: in 1817, a country village in Surrey, a few miles south of London. At one time noted for its mineral waters, it was popular as a retreat from the city pollution and therefore a good place to establish a school for young ladies.

31 *Library Subscription book*: the hub of the seaside resort at this time, the library, a private institution, would be subscribed to by all genteel visitors whether or not they were keen readers. Its register of book lenders would therefore act as a social directory. The entries so far (banal names and lowly occupations) suggest that Sanditon is not yet attracting a distinguished set.

32 *Camilla*: *Camilla; or, A Picture of Youth* (1796), the second novel of Frances Burney (1752–1840). Its heroine, Camilla Tyrold, just seventeen, has many misadventures, including overspending on keepsakes and clothing on her visit to the fashionable spa town of Tunbridge Wells. JA greatly admired Burney, one of the most esteemed writers of the day, acknowledging her in a famous passage in *Northanger Abbey* (1818), ch. 5, on the importance of the novel genre. JA's copy of *Camilla* is now in the Bodleian Library, Oxford.

35 *French Boarding School*: run by a French woman or a woman purporting to be French, like Mrs La Tournelle (actually Sarah Hackitt) who ran the Abbey House School in Reading attended by JA and her sister Cassandra in the mid 1780s. From the late eighteenth century, boarding schools were an increasingly popular choice for the education of girls of wealthy families.

Asses milk: easily digested, it was recommended for those suffering from a variety of ailments, including asthma and consumption (tuberculosis). Motherby recommends it as an 'antispasmodicum' (against convulsions) (*New Medical Dictionary*, 94).

Chamber-Horse: 'a piece of exercise equipment which simulates the motion of horse riding, typically consisting of a sprung chair on which the user sits and bounces up and down' (*OED*).

39 *Man of Feeling*: possibly an allusion to the novel by Henry Mackenzie (1745–1831), *The Man of Feeling* (1771), with its hyper-sensitive hero, incapacitated for normal living by his exquisite feelings. If so, Sir Edward Denham, with his clichéd responses, is a ludicrous caricature of the literary type.

either of Scott's Poems: by 1817, Walter Scott (1771–1832), the best-selling poet of the age, had published many more than two poems. *OED*, sense 4c, records 'either' meaning 'any one (of more than two)'; but JA probably refers here to the two of Scott's poems scantily quoted from by Sir Edward Denham a few lines later: *Marmion* (1808), canto 6, verse 30 ('O, Woman! In our hours of ease') and *The Lady of the Lake* (1810), canto 2, verse 22 ('Some feelings are to mortals given').

Burns Lines to his Mary: Robert Burns (1759–96), whose love poems to Mary Campbell ('Highland Mary') are probably referred to here: 'The Highland Lassie O', 'Will ye go to the Indies, my Mary', and, after her early death, 'To Mary in Heaven'. By the early nineteenth century, the 'irregularities' of Burns's character (sex and drink), referred to by Charlotte

Heywood a few lines later, had been much biographized and conflated with the sentiments expressed in his poetry.

Montgomery . . . Wordsworth . . . Campbell: contemporary poets James Montgomery (1771–1854); William Wordsworth (1770–1850); Thomas Campbell (1777–1844), whose *The Pleasures of Hope* (1799), Part 2, line 224, is quoted here. Given Sir Edward's inability to recall more than a line from poems he claims to adore, this is probably no more than a checklist, as likely gleaned from the ample reviews in the journals of the day as from reading specific works. Curious by its omission from the list is any reference to the poetry of Lord Byron (1788–1824). Later writers attempting to continue JA's novel bring out Sir Edward's obvious Byronic features—notably his 'danger' to women.

43 *a Co-*: a co-heiress, sharing her inheritance with at least one other person.

Landed or Funded: Lady Denham is distinguishing the real gentry, whose status derived from land and its income or from money invested in government stocks, from those who, engaged in one of the professions (generally socially inferior), relied on salaries.

Half pay officers: officers in the navy and army not currently in active service.

Jointure: property settled on a woman at marriage, to be used when her husband has died. Although Lady Denham, in possession of unusual independent wealth, seems to scorn such provision, it could be a source of great enjoyment, as Mrs Jennings proves in JA's first published novel, *Sense and Sensibility* (1811).

45 *Alembic*: an apparatus used for distilling chemicals, the term also had a recognized figurative use. In this case, the suggestion of a scientific test for extracting literary nuggets from trashy novels contributes nothing meaningful to Sir Edward's nonsensical use of language.

46 *indomptible . . . anti-puerile*: examples of Sir Edward's addiction, as Charlotte Heywood expresses it, 'to all the newest-fashioned hard words' (p. 41). Here he peppers his vocabulary with yet more 'anti-' and 'pseudo-' words. 'Indomptible' is JA's spelling for 'indomptable', listed in *OED* as a rare or obsolete form of 'indomitable' (meaning 'unyielding', 'resolute'). The surviving manuscript shows that, like 'anti-puerile' later in his speech, the word was a revision, as JA deliberately heightened Sir Edward's language to make it more bizarre ('indomptible' replacing the tamer 'unconquerable', 'anti-puerile' replacing 'sagacious'). 'Eleemosynary' is a hard word for 'charitable'. The repetition of 'high-toned' (in 'high-toned Machinations'), when earlier he claimed for Burns 'the soul of high toned Genius' (p. 40), may hint at the narrow range of Sir Edward's hard words.

47 *Richardson's . . . Lovelaces*: the reader already knows that Sir Edward has read too many improbable romances and fancies his sex appeal is irresistible. Here JA ties down his character more firmly: he models himself on Robert Lovelace, the seducer and eventual rapist of Clarissa Harlowe, heroine of Samuel Richardson's extremely long novel-in-letters, *Clarissa, or, The*

Explanatory Notes

al for

History of a Young Lady (1747–8). Richardson (1689–1761) was a favourite with JA, but she was not above making fun of his morally complex (even ambiguous) work and the crudely melodramatic fictions replete with rakish anti-heroes that it spawned.

47 *Tombuctoo*: Timbuctoo, in present-day Mali, on the edge of the Sahara Desert, but meaning here simply a sufficiently remote place. In the spoof 'Plan of a Novel, according to hints from various quarters', probably written in spring 1816, JA imagined a heroine who, fleeing from the alarming advances of an 'anti-hero', is 'compelled to retreat into Kamschatka' (modern Kamchatka, a peninsula in the Russian far east) (see 'Plan of a Novel', in *Minor Works*, ed. R. W. Chapman (1954); rev. B. C. Southam (Oxford: Oxford University Press, 1969), 430). She was ridiculing the improbable settings of some contemporary novels, like Sophie Cottin's *Elizabeth; or, The Exiles of Siberia* (1806) and Mary Brunton's *Self-Control* (1810). In Brunton's novel, the heroine is kidnapped from London by her would-be seducer and confined among Indians in the wilds of Canada before she eventually escapes by canoe.

49 *Post Horses*: hired horses changed at regular 'posts' or inns to maximize speed of travel.

50 *Seminary*: 'In the earlier half of the 19th cent. "Seminary for Young Ladies" was very common as the designation of a private school for girls' (*OED*, sense 4).

55 *Projector*: Johnson, *Dictionary*, sense 1: 'One who forms schemes or designs'; sense 2: 'One who forms wild impracticable schemes'.

56 *Lusty*: 'corpulent, stout, fat' (*OED*, sense 10, with a first reference to such usage, 1777).

57 *Hack-Chaises*: hired carriages, like taxis.

59 *Physics*: natural sciences in general.

60 *Coats of the Stomach*: a medical term, referring to the four protective membrane layers lining the stomach.

64 *half-mulatto*: mulatto 'a person having one white and one black parent . . . of mixed race' (*OED*). Miss Lambe presumably therefore has one black grandparent and is perhaps the child of a plantation owner and a freed slave. The term 'mulatto', though now offensive, appears elsewhere in the literature of the period. JA's use of 'half-mulatto' is, however, unusual.

65 *Tonic Pills*: a patent medicine with investors, like Mrs Griffiths's cousin, in the business of their manufacture and sale.

68 *Charitable Repository*: a kind of charity shop from which donated goods were sold for the benefit of the poor.

69 *Gig . . . Pheaton . . . Tandem*: a gig was a light, two-wheeled open carriage drawn by a single horse; a phaeton had four wheels, was drawn by a pair of horses, and had one or two seats facing forwards; a tandem was two-wheeled with two horses harnessed one behind the other.

70 *paling*: a fence made from wooden pales or stakes.

The Oxford World's Classics Website

www.worldsclassics.co.uk

- Browse the full range of Oxford World's Classics online

- Sign up for our monthly e-alert to receive information on new titles

- Read extracts from the Introductions

- Listen to our editors and translators talk about the world's greatest literature with our Oxford World's Classics audio guides

- Join the conversation, follow us on Twitter at OWC_Oxford

- Teachers and lecturers can order inspection copies quickly and simply via our website

www.worldsclassics.co.uk

ANTHONY TROLLOPE

The American Senator
An Autobiography
Barchester Towers
Can You Forgive Her?
Cousin Henry
Doctor Thorne
The Duke's Children
The Eustace Diamonds
Framley Parsonage
He Knew He Was Right
Lady Anna
The Last Chronicle of Barset
Orley Farm
Phineas Finn
Phineas Redux
The Prime Minister
Rachel Ray
The Small House at Allington
The Warden
The Way We Live Now